La Nouvelle Pâtisserie

La Nouvelle Pâtisserie

THE ART & SCIENCE
OF MAKING BEAUTIFUL
PASTRIES & DESSERTS

· · ·  · · ·

Jean-Yves Duperret
and
Jacqueline Mallorca

VIKING

VIKING
Published by the Penguin Group
Viking Penguin Inc., 40 West 23rd Street,
New York, New York 10010, U.S.A.
Penguin Books Ltd, 27 Wrights Lane,
London W8 5TZ, England
Penguin Books Australia Ltd, Ringwood,
Victoria, Australia
Penguin Books Canada Ltd, 2801 John Street,
Markham, Ontario, Canada L3R 1B4
Penguin Books (N.Z.) Ltd, 182-190 Wairau Road,
Auckland 10, New Zealand

Penguin Books Ltd, Registered Offices:
Harmondsworth, Middlesex, England

First published in 1988 by Viking Penguin Inc.
Published simultaneously in Canada

1 3 5 7 9 10 8 6 4 2

LIBRARY OF CONGRESS CATALOGING IN PUBLICATION DATA
Duperret, Jean-Yves.
La Nouvelle Pâtisserie.
Includes index.
1. Pastry. 2. Desserts. I. Mallorca,
Jacqueline. II. Title. III. Title: La Nouvelle
Pâtisserie.
TX773.D82   1988   641.8'65   87-40439
ISBN 0-670-81550-0

Printed in the United States of America by
Arcata Graphics, Fairfield, Pennsylvania
Set in Baskerville and Snell Roundhand
Designed by Beth Tondreau Design
Illustrations by Jacqueline Mallorca
Photographs by Thomas Lindley

Contents

. . . ◇ . . .

Foreword

. . . ◊ . . .

Unlike most French pastry chefs, who start their apprenticeship at a very early age, Jean-Yves Duperret found his chosen career almost by accident. He was studying to be an electrical engineer when he met and married his wife, Nelly, who was attending law school in Tours, the couple's hometown. His new father-in-law owned a bakery there, and Jean-Yves started helping with the business. He soon became deeply interested in the work and within two years was traveling around France in order to enter professional pastry competitions. He later studied with some of France's top *pâtissiers*, including Gaston Lenôtre, and he and Nelly seriously considered opening a pastry shop in Paris. Instead, they opted to move to the United States in 1980 with their young son, Alexis, and settled in San Francisco. After a period of three years, during which Jean-Yves taught *pâtisserie* classes at The California Culinary Academy and did private catering, they opened their first California bakery on Union Street, *La Nouvelle Pâtisserie*. It was an immediate success, and a number of branches were soon to follow; one is now planned for New York City.

Preface

· · · ◇ · · ·

This book was written for you, the home cook, because it was people just like you who convinced me that it needed to be written. It was an evolutionary process: First, there were personal requests and letters from customers who had visited my bakery in San Francisco, asking for recipes and inquiring if I gave cooking classes, and then, the resultant evening classes progressed into three-day teaching seminars, and finally this volume became a reality.

The main goal of this book is to simplify the complex techniques of pastry making and to "demystify" the whole process so that you can make beautiful cakes and pastries in your own kitchen. I do emphasize using only the finest and freshest ingredients—it is impossible to skimp or substitute—but you do not have to acquire a lot of professional bakers' equipment. In these pages you will find many suggestions for creative alternatives that will help you achieve good results. For example, I explain how to simulate a baker's proofing cupboard for raising yeast doughs with a cardboard box and a pan of boiling water, and how to use the rim of an ordinary springform pan as a professional baker's cake ring. I do recommend, though, that you have a candy thermometer and a scale for consistently good results, but these are not major investments.

In many ways it is easier for the home cook who is learning about the art of *pâtisserie* to work successfully here than it would be in France, because the basic ingredients available here are of such consistently high quality. For instance, in France flour can vary considerably from sack to sack. This is because there are many small farmers, and milling procedures are not standardized. This affects baking techniques. For example, here in the United States my croissant or puff dough is very soft and supple and much easier to work with than it was in France. There, my dough had to be firmer, and required adjustment each time according to the quality of the flour. This takes a great deal of experience. As a matter of fact, when I came to this country I found that American flour, butter, and cream all reacted differently from those I had been used to. I had to readjust all my recipes and learn how to control my American ingredients precisely. In the process, I developed some very useful new techniques, which I hope you will find to your benefit.

The recipes in these pages have been presented in a simple and logical way, so that even the most exotic of desserts can be assembled in a step-by-step process, and I have shared many, many professional tips for achieving the very best results possible. I enjoyed creating this book—it is my heartfelt hope that you thoroughly enjoy using it.

Jean-Yves Duperret
San Francisco, 1988

La Nouvelle Pâtisserie

Ingredients

· · · ◊ · · ·

Most of the ingredients called for in this book will be familiar to the average cook, but a few deserve further explanation in the context of pastry making.

ALMOND MEAL, ALMONDS   Almond meal is another term for powdered almonds, an ingredient used extensively in pâtisserie. Though it is available in bulk to professional bakers, home cooks usually have to grind their own. Unless color is important, as in marzipan or almond paste, the skins may be left on the nuts. (To blanch almonds, drop in boiling water for 1 minute, then drain. When almonds are cool enough to be handled, pop the nuts out of the skins.) Most United States supermarkets sell blanched slivered almonds and unblanched sliced almonds.

ALMOND PASTE   Virtually the same as marzipan, almond paste is made of ground blanched almonds, sugar and/or glucose, and egg whites. True almond paste does not have more than fifty percent sugar.

ANGELICA   Popular in France and England with confectioners and pâtissiers, angelica is the candied root of an aromatic herb, *Angelica archangelica*. Light green in color, it has a delicate but distinctive flavor. It is available in specialty food shops and is usually imported from France.

BAKING POWDER, BAKING SODA   Like yeast, baking powder and baking soda (bicarbonate of soda; sodium bicarbonate) are used for leavening, but do not require rising time. Baking powder is generally used with mild-tasting, alkaline ingredients, while baking soda must be balanced by some acidic ingredient, such as molasses or buttermilk, to avoid a soapy taste. When mixed with a dough, double-acting baking powder releases a small amount of its gases at room temperature but most are given off in the second rising, in the heat of the oven. Be sure that your baking powder is fresh; it can lose its raising power if stored for too long.

BUTTER Salt is a preservative, so unsalted butter is the best choice when making cakes, pastry, and confectionery, as it is invariably fresher and therefore has a better flavor. If salt is required, it can then be added to taste. Lightly salted butter is perfectly acceptable when a little sodium is required to heighten flavors. It is advisable to buy butter from a store with a rapid turnover; salt can mask the flavor of rancid butter. Always use unsalted butter for buttercreams.

CHOCOLATE In pâtisserie, dark (also known as bitter, bittersweet, or semisweet) milk, and white chocolates are used extensively. Unsweetened dark chocolate, as the name implies, contains no sugar at all. It is best to buy chocolate with a very high cocoa butter content (it is always the most expensive), as it is the smoothest, has the richest flavor, and will give the best results.

DÉCORS A few recipes in this book, such as the marzipan acorns, mention chocolate décors. Also known as chocolate sprinkles, these tiny sticks are used for cake decoration and will be found in most United States supermarkets in the baking ingredients/decoration section. In the same department will be found the small silver balls sometimes known as dragées in France and the United Kingdom. They are edible, and are made of sugar.

EGGS The eggs sold commercially in the United States are graded from peewee to jumbo. The recipes in this book were all tested with large eggs, at 2 ounces each or 24 ounces to the dozen.

FILBERTS *See* hazelnuts

FLOUR All the recipes in this book have been tested with regular all-purpose flour, which should always be weighed first and then sifted. It gives excellent results. However, bread flour, pastry flour, and cake flour may be used where appropriate, if preferred. (Hard-wheat bread flour has an extra-high gluten content; pastry or cake flour has an extra-low gluten content.)

HAZELNUTS These roundish, sweet-flavored nuts are less readily available than almonds or pecans in the United States, but can usually be found in health food stores. To remove the skins, spread the nuts out on a baking sheet and toast in 350°F. oven for 20 minutes, and then rub the nuts together in a kitchen towel.

MARZIPAN A paste made from ground almonds, sugar and/or glucose, and egg whites, this is used both as a confection and in cakes and pastries. It is available commercially, but a superior-quality product can easily be made in the home kitchen (recipe, page 243). When used for modeling, such as fashioning marzipan roses or leaves, it should have fondant or confectioners' sugar added so that it will hold its shape.

ORANGE FLOWER WATER Distilled from orange blossoms and much used in French pâtisserie, this fragrant flavoring is available at specialty food stores. It is usually imported from France. If unavailable, substitute orange extract.

SUGAR The cane sugar generally used in pâtisserie includes regular granulated white sugar, light and dark brown sugar (with molasses added), and confectioners', or powdered, white sugar, which contains a small amount of cornstarch. Coarse sugar crystals, or "pearl" sugar, are used for decoration on some cookies and choux pastries.

YEAST Baker's fresh compressed yeast, which is sold in ⅗-ounce cakes in some supermarkets, is preferable to the dried granular yeast generally available, as it gives better results. It must be kept under refrigeration. A ⅗-ounce cake of fresh yeast is the equivalent of a ¼-ounce package of dried granular yeast.

Equipment

. . . ◊ . . .

The professional pastry chef uses surprisingly few pieces of kitchen equipment, and most of these are both inexpensive and readily available. Of course, in my bakery kitchen I do have some large items, such as proofing boxes with controlled heat and humidity for raising yeast doughs, big convection ovens, multishelved freezers and refrigerators, pastry dough rolling machines, and heavy-duty mixers of very large capacity. However, these are for producing cakes and pastries in volume. All my smaller items, such as cake pans, molds, pastry rings, baking sheets, and so on, are identical to those that can be purchased in any good kitchenware shop.

I have described only those items that relate to specific recipes in this book; naturally there are a great many more available. I have not mentioned standard items, such as bowls, knives, whisks, sieves, and wooden spoons, as they are common to every kitchen. If you do not already own a scale, I urgently recommend that you acquire one. Cakes and pastries have a habit of not turning out well if the proportions are incorrect, and it is impossible to get consistent results without measuring the ingredients precisely.

BABA MOLDS These come in two shapes: bucket-shaped timbales and miniature ring molds. The former are easier to fill with dough, and can be used for savory timbales as well as babas au rhum. Usually made of tinned steel or aluminum, the 2-inch deep, 3-ounce size is the most useful for the home kitchen.

BAKER'S COOLING RACKS Cakes, cookies, and breads should be cooled on a raised grid when they come out of the oven, otherwise trapped steam on the underside will make them soggy. In the home kitchen, it's best to have at least two, of stainless steel wire. They should be slightly bigger than a half-sheet baking pan: about 20 by 12 inches, so that you can cool sheet cakes.

BAKER'S LONG FLEXIBLE SPATULA *See* pastry spatula

BAKING PARCHMENT This is sold in large sheets or in rolls, like plastic wrap, and is especially treated for use in the oven. Use it to line baking sheets: it eliminates greasing and flouring them and therefore saves a great deal of time. Sheet cakes, cookies, and various pastries will unmold easily, and the paper can be wiped off and reused if no batter has stuck to it. Baking parchment is also used for making disposable paper decorating cones, and for cooking fish and poultry en papillote, or in a paper case.

BAKING SHEETS The most versatile baking sheet for home use is undoubtedly the professional, heavy aluminum half-sheet baking pan, which gets its name from the fact that it bakes a sheet cake half the size of a standard bakery sheet cake. (A full-size pan will not fit in most domestic ovens.) It measures 17 by 12 by 1 inches and can be used for a sheet cake; a jelly roll or a biscuit roulade; cookies; yeast rolls; breads; and as a tray for holding small molds, pastry rings, and so on, in the oven. It is convenient to own at least two.

BRIOCHE MOLDS Traditionally used for brioches (recipe, page 87), these widely flared, fluted molds are usually made of tinned steel. You can use the large sizes (8- to 9½-inch diameter) as a mold for an attractive charlotte by lining the flutes with ladyfingers and filling the center with a gelatin-enriched custard. The standard individual-sized brioche mold holds 4 ounces.

CAKE BOARDS All professional pastry chefs use cake boards when assembling cakes, as they make it easy to pick up both layers and assembled cakes. They are simply circles or rectangles of corrugated cardboard with a moisture-resistant surface, and come in a wide range of sizes. If they are unobtainable, you can make them with ordinary cardboard cut to size and covered with aluminum foil.

CAKE PANS, round, 8 inches and 9 inches in diameter and 2 inches high. I prefer the extra-heavy tinned steel pans of one-piece construction, as they bake evenly. If you first brush them generously with soft butter you will never have difficulty unmolding your cakes. Heavy aluminum is my next choice.

CAKE PANS, square, 8 by 8 by 1 inches. Tinned steel and heavy aluminum are the best materials.

CAKE RINGS These are simply bands of steel that pastry chefs use for assembling cakes with delicate fillings that have to "set up," or jell, in the refrigerator. The most useful sizes are 8 inches and 9 inches in diameter and 2 inches high. I use 6 inches in diameter and 3½ inches high for proofing and baking Italian panettone, which is a tall, cylindrical fruit loaf.

CANDY THERMOMETER This is used for measuring the different stages through which sugar passes as it heats, from a syrup at 215°F. to caramel at 350°F. This thermometer is also useful for judging the readiness of delicate custards, such as Crème Anglaise, which turn grainy if overcooked. Most models register from 100° to 400°F. and are made of stainless steel and glass.

CHARLOTTE MOLD This simple mold has very slightly flared sides and twin handles, which are useful when turning out hot fruit charlottes or chilled custard creams; they can also be used for baking cylindrical loaves. A 1-quart mold is usual for general home use.

CHOCOLATE THERMOMETER Chocolate must be tempered in order to have a proper sheen when used to cover cakes and candy. This involves heating and cooling at precise temperatures from 80° to 122°F. (see page 241 for details), which is below the range on a candy thermometer. The chocolate thermometer, which consists of a long glass tube with a mercury bubble, measures from 50° to 140°F. in 1° gradations.

COPPER SUGAR PAN Made for professional use of extra-heavy, solid copper, these pans are left unlined because they are intended *only* for cooking sugar. (Unlike many other, more acidic foods, sugar does not interact with copper.) As this metal conducts heat extremely well, sugar will melt easily in such a pan and be much easier to control as it passes through various stages, from simple syrup to dark caramel. (See notes on cooking sugar, page 237.) These pans have a good-sized pouring spout and a sturdy handle, which is invariably also of copper. It is good practice *always* to lay a folded towel over the handle when using the pan, to remind yourself that it will become very hot. If you don't have such a pan, boil sugar in stainless steel—the high temperatures realized when cooking sugar can damage other materials, such as enameled iron, and will melt the lining off a tin-lined copper pan.

DECORATING COMB Used for cake decoration, the comb is drawn lightly across buttercream or chocolate frostings to create straight or wavy parallel lines. A flat aluminum triangle, it has serrated edges of three different sizes: fine, medium, and coarse.

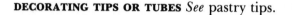

DECORATING TIPS OR TUBES *See* pastry tips.

ELECTRIC STAND MIXER While not absolutely essential, a good mixer does provide excellent results when it comes to aerating mixtures, making buttercreams, or kneading doughs. The best American-made model for home use has a powerful motor with variable speeds and comes with a flat K-shaped beater, a large balloon whisk, a dough hook, and a deep stainless steel bowl. This is invaluable, as you can use it over a pan of simmering water when preparing cake batters that require gentle heat before being transferred to the stand for beating and aerating until cold. Get the most powerful model available; it does a better job on bread doughs.

FOOD PROCESSOR In the pastry kitchen, this versatile machine is particularly useful for preparing Praliné Paste, Marzipan, and certain cookie and pastry doughs, and for puréeing fruit fillings and combining sugar syrups with fruit mixtures.

KUGELHOPF MOLD This large fluted pan is used for baking the yeast-raised Austrian sweet bread of the same name, which imitates a turkish turban. Usually made of tinned steel or aluminum, it has a central tube to promote even baking.

LOAF/BREAD PANS I use these rectangular pans for baking some of the plain cakes in Chapter 7 and for Christmas fruitcakes. Tinned steel and heavy aluminum give the best results.

NUT MILL/NUT GRINDER An old-fashioned, hand-cranked nut mill of enameled iron and tinned steel grinds nuts into fine flakes or nut meal. Electric food processors and blenders, on the other hand, chop nuts into granules and release the oil, which is not always desirable. Though small, they are fast to use and adequate for the home kitchen. (Professional bakers are able to buy fine-textured nut meal in bulk.) I prefer to use a very fine nut meal in cakes, as it gives lighter results.

OVEN THERMOMETER As any chef who has ever given cooking demonstrations on tour will confirm, oven thermostats are notorious for their inaccuracy! Small portable oven thermometers, usually made of stainless steel and glass, are very inexpensive. I recommend that you buy one and check your home oven periodically, and make any necessary adjustments when baking. Many home ovens are off by at least 25°. If you are fortunate enough to have a convection oven, you will find that it bakes faster and more efficiently than the regular type. To compensate, reduce the temperature specified in recipes by 25°F. and start checking for doneness 10 minutes before stated baking time is up.

PASTRY AND DECORATING TIPS OR TUBES Of tinned steel, these cone-shaped nozzles are available in a great variety of sizes. For general purposes, you will need a ¼-inch and a ½-inch plain round tip and two star tips, one "closed" and one "open." These large tips are used without a coupling, whereas small decorating tips require a plastic collar to hold them in place.

PASTRY BAGS These cone-shaped bags are used with pastry tips of various sizes for forming choux paste and certain cookies, and for decorating purposes. Usually made from nylon or plastic-coated cotton, they should be washed and hung up to dry as soon as possible after use or they become sticky and difficult to clean. It is advisable to have at least three 12-inch to 14-inch pastry bags.

PASTRY CRIMPER/PINCER Shaped like simple tweezers, but broader, the inside tips are ridged. To make a decorative edge on the rim of

a tart, the crimper is lightly closed on
the pastry at a slight angle, at
equal intervals.

PASTRY CUTTERS Made of heavy tinned steel for professional use,
these come boxed in sets of nine or ten, in graduated sizes. For
general use I recommend two sets of round cutters, plain and fluted,
from about ¾ inch to 4½ inches in diameter.

PASTRY GUIDES These are pairs of wooden rules that are used in
conjunction with a rolling pin to produce evenly rolled dough. They
are placed on either side of the dough, and the rolling pin is run
across them, flattening the dough to the height of the rules. They
are invaluable for novice pastry makers. Make your own from scrap
lumber: ⅛, ¼, and ½ inch thick by 18 inches long.

PASTRY/DOUGH SCRAPER This rectangular metal blade is
used for picking up and mixing sticky
or delicate doughs, and for working
chocolate and fondant. It is especially
useful for cleaning off butcherblock surfaces.
Those made of stainless steel with a rolled hollow
handle are preferable.

PASTRY SPATULA/BAKER'S FLEXIBLE SPATULA
This tool, with its long narrow blade, is
used for spreading batters in sheet cake pans,
and for applying and smoothing cake
frostings and fillings. Both the flat and
offset handle types are usually made
of stainless steel. A 9-inch or 10-inch
blade is convenient.

PASTRY/TART RINGS Also known as flan rings, these are available in sizes from 3½ inches to 10¼ inches in diameter and ⅝ inches deep. Made of stainless steel, they are placed on baking sheets and used to support open-faced tarts as they bake.

PLASTIC SCRAPER Somewhat like a very large plastic or rubber spatula without a handle, this useful bowl scraper/mixing tool is also invaluable for filling pastry bags.

QUICHE PAN/TART PAN with removable base. An alternative to the pastry ring, these tinned steel pans have fluted sides and are available in a wide range of sizes, from the individual 4-inch ones to about 10 inches in diameter. To unmold the baked tart, the base is pushed up from underneath, or the pan can be set down on a can and the rim allowed to fall down. The baked tart can be left on the base or not, as you please.

ROLLING PIN I prefer the classic straight rolling pin of dense hardwood, about 19 inches long and 2 inches in diameter, which gives you a good "feel" of the dough under your hands. As it has no handles, you are less likely to rock it from side to side, which promotes uneven dough.

SALAMANDER This tool gets its name from the lizard, which doesn't mind intense heat! Somewhat like a branding iron, it consists of a thick iron disk on a long stem with a wooden handle. It is heated on top of the stove, and is used for melting a thin layer of sugar on top of certain custards and soufflés to form a brittle caramelized layer.

SAVARIN MOLD This tinned steel seamless ring of 8 to $9\frac{1}{2}$ inches in diameter is used for baking the yeast-raised ring cake of the same name. It is shallower and wider than the standard ring mold.

SCALE I cannot recommend too strongly the use of scales when baking—it is an exact science. There are several different types available: spring balance, beam balance, digital, and the old-fashioned kind with weights. Today, most show both ounces and grams. Choose one that is easy to read, with a pan from which you can pour dry ingredients conveniently. Also, make sure that the total weight capacity suits your needs—one that holds 10 ounces won't require much counter space but is of limited use when measuring flour for bread or puff paste.

SPRINGFORM PAN This pan is made up of two parts, with the base separate from the sides. In most cases the base fits into a groove running around the bottom of the rim, or sides. The rim has a clamp release to facilitate the unmolding of delicate cakes that cannot be turned upside down.

Equivalent Weights & Measures

. . . ◇ . . .

To get consistent results, it is strongly recommended that the ingredients for all the recipes in this book be weighed, but as cup measures are commonly used in the United States, these have been included as well. Remember that the volume of different ingredients can vary dramatically: a cup of flour does not weigh the same as a cup of sugar.

Metric measurements are listed for the benefit of European readers, and have been taken to the nearest convenient equivalent. To convert ounces to grams, multiply ounces by 28.35. To convert grams to ounces, multiply by .035.

ALMOND MEAL (powdered or ground almonds)

½ ounce	2 tablespoons	15 grams
1 ounce	¼ cup	30 grams
2 ounces	½ cup	55 grams
4 ounces	1 cup	115 grams

ALMONDS (whole), HAZELNUTS (whole)

2 ounces	⅓ cup	55 grams
4 ounces	⅔ cup	115 grams
6 ounces	1 cup	170 grams

COCOA, Dutch process, unsweetened, powder

½ ounce	2 tablespoons	15 grams
1 ounce	¼ cup	30 grams

COFFEE, instant espresso, powder

½ ounce	¼ cup	15 grams
1 ounce	½ cup	30 grams
2 ounces	1 cup	55 grams

CONFECTIONERS' SUGAR, unsifted volume

½ ounce	2½ tablespoons	15 grams
1 ounce	¼ cup	30 grams
2 ounces	½ cup	55 grams
4 ounces	1 cup	115 grams
8 ounces	2 cups	230 grams

EGGS, large

1 whole egg	2 ounces	55 grams
1 egg yolk	¾ ounce	20 grams
1 egg white	1¼ ounces	35 grams
4 egg whites	5 ounces	140 grams
13 egg whites	16¼ ounces/ 1 pint plus	450 grams

FLOUR, all-purpose, unsifted volume

½ ounce	2 tablespoons	15 grams
1 ounce	¼ cup	30 grams
2 ounces	½ cup, scant	55 grams
3 ounces	⅔ cup, scant	80 grams
3½ ounces	⅔ cup, generous	95 grams
4 ounces	¾ cup, scant	115 grams
4½ ounces	⅞ cup, scant	130 grams
5 ounces	1 cup, scant	140 grams
5½ ounces	1 cup plus 2 tablespoons	155 grams
6 ounces	1¼ cups, scant	170 grams
6½ ounces	1¼ cups, generous	185 grams
7 ounces	1⅓ cups	200 grams
7½ ounces	1½ cups, scant	215 grams
8 ounces	1½ cups	230 grams
10 ounces	2 cups	280 grams
15 ounces	3 cups, scant	420 grams
1 pound	3¼ cups	450 grams

GELATIN, unflavored granules

¼ ounce	2 teaspoons (1 envelope)	7½ grams
½ ounce	4 teaspoons	15 grams

RAISINS, CURRANTS, DICED CANDIED PEEL

2 ounces	⅓ cup	55 grams
6 ounces	1 cup	170 grams
12 ounces	2 cups	340 grams

SUGAR, white, granulated

½ ounce	1 tablespoon	15 grams
1 ounce	2 tablespoons	30 grams
2 ounces	¼ cup, generous	55 grams
3 ounces	⅓ cup, generous	80 grams

3½ ounces	½ cup, scant	95 grams
4 ounces	½ cup	115 grams
4½ ounces	½ cup, generous	130 grams
5 ounces	⅔ cup, scant	140 grams
5½ ounces	⅔ cup	155 grams
6 ounces	¾ cup, scant	170 grams
6½ ounces	¾ cup	185 grams
7 ounces	¾ cup, generous	200 grams
7½ ounces	1 cup	215 grams
8 ounces	1 cup, generous	230 grams

WALNUT PIECES and PECAN PIECES

1 ounce	¼ cup	30 grams
2 ounces	½ cup	55 grams

CONVERSION OF LIQUID MEASURES To convert quarts to liters, multiply by 1.057. To convert liters to quarts, multiply by .95. One deciliter equals 6⅔ tablespoons. One tablespoon equals ½ liquid ounce, or 15 grams.

CONVERSION OF LINEAR MEASURES To convert inches to centimeters, multiply the inch by 2.54. To convert centimeters to inches, multiply the centimeter by .39.

¼ inch	¾ centimeter
½ inch	1½ centimeters
1 inch	2½ centimeters
8 inches	20 centimeters
9 inches	23 centimeters
10 inches	25 centimeters

CONVERSION OF TEMPERATURES To convert Fahrenheit degrees to Celsius, subtract 32, multiply by 5, and divide by 9. To convert Celsius to Fahrenheit, multiply by 9, divide by 5, and add 32. Celsius and Centigrade are the same.

212°F.	100°C.
250°F.	120°C.
300°F.	150°C.
350°F.	180°C.
400°F.	205°C.

1.

Sugar Doughs (Pâte Brisée) & Tarts

· · · ◇ · · ·

Tarts are among the easiest as well as the most popular preparations in a pastry cook's repertoire, but they are also the most delicate and do not keep well. They should be enjoyed as soon as possible after baking, so that the pastry shell remains crisp in contrast to the texture of the filling.

I usually bake several tarts at a time, in straight-sided pastry rings set on a baking sheet. The pastry shells brown well, and it is a simple matter to lift off the rings. Naturally, you can use a shallow metal quiche pan with a loose base and fluted sides if you prefer.

In a top-class professional bakery, the dough generally used for tarts is known as pâte brisée, pâte à tarte, or pâte à foncer (short, rich tart pastry or lining paste). Richer pastry is known as pâte sucrée (sweet short pastry or sugar dough). These mixtures are very close to being cookie doughs, and in fact any scraps and leftovers can be rolled, cut, and baked to make cookies.

While I do not use it professionally, as it cannot be made successfully in large quantities, I have included a recipe for a good and very easy Food Processor Pâte Brisée, which can be assembled in two minutes and used almost immediately. Short and tender, it is excellent if baked and served at once. (I prefer to use a dough containing eggs if a tart has to wait for a few hours.)

You may be surprised to discover that when I make sugar doughs, I mix the sugar, eggs, lemon juice, and warm-room-temperature butter together and then add the flour, mixing it in quickly. The resulting even-textured dough is soft, and must be well chilled before rolling, but it is very quick to prepare and bakes most successfully. Also, it never gets too hard to roll, even when well chilled. In my professional kitchen I use an electric mixer when preparing large quantities of this dough, but I recommend that you make all doughs by hand a few times (beat ingredients together with a pastry whisk) so that you develop a good "feel"—the hallmark of all successful pastry cooks.

Mix and handle pastry doughs as lightly as possible—overhandling makes them elastic and tough—and remember that your refrigerator is as important as your oven. Cold butter holds flour and sugar efficiently, and your pastry will then bake crisply. Warm butter, on the other hand, will melt immediately in a hot oven and the dough will spread itself out sadly. Therefore, I urge you to chill your doughs after mixing, and again after lining your pastry rings. Incidentally, prepared pastry shells can go straight from the freezer to the oven.

In order for tart shells to bake evenly, the dough must be rolled to exactly the same thickness, which takes practice. The easiest way to get consistent results when you first start working with pastry dough is to roll it between two wooden sticks placed about 12 inches apart on your lightly floured work surface. (Too much flour will make your pastry heavy.) Keep three sets of pastry guides handy: $1/8$, $1/4$, and $1/2$ inch thick and about 18 inches long.

I recommend using a long, straight hardwood rolling pin of professional weight and quality—you get a better feel of the dough under your hands, and you cannot rock this type of pin from side to side, making the dough uneven. Always work with a generous amount of dough, as it is difficult to roll skimpy quantities properly. Excess dough will keep in the refrigerator for three days or more, and can be frozen, properly wrapped, for up to two months. Incidentally, many of the tarts in this chapter are delicious made with puff dough instead of sugar dough: see page 72 for directions on forming a puff paste shell.

Some tart recipes call for a prebaked pastry shell. In spite of what your grandmother (and my grandmother) and various culinary authorities may have told you, it is perfectly possible to bake a pastry shell without wasting time lining and filling it with paper and dried beans. If you follow my technique exactly the sides will not fall down.

To prebake a sugar dough shell without a filling:

Preheat oven to 400°F. Butter a 9-inch pastry ring. Line a baking sheet with baking parchment and place the ring on it. On a lightly floured surface, roll dough out ⅛ inch thick. Work it into a circle about 3 inches larger than your pastry ring, lightly "flapping" and rotating the dough to make sure that it does not stick. Dust very lightly with flour as you work. Pick up dough on your rolling pin and center it over pastry ring. Form a "pouch" against the sides of the ring by pushing dough with the fingertips of one upturned hand while lightly attaching it to the rim with the thumb of the other hand (see illustration). Run rolling pin across ring to cut off excess dough. Flatten this "pouch" with your thumbs, so that ¼ inch of dough stands above the rim. Using pastry pincers held at an angle, form a decorative edge, which should extend ⅛ inch above the rim. Run your finger around the inside, exerting a very slight pressure, so that a tiny lip of pastry rests on top of the rim. This will prevent the sides of your pastry shell from falling down as it bakes, but don't overdo it, or the baked shell will break when you remove the ring. Prick bottom of shell well and freeze for 10 minutes. Bake for 20 minutes, or until golden brown. Check after 5 minutes to make sure that the bottom of shell hasn't formed an air bubble. If so, quickly deflate with

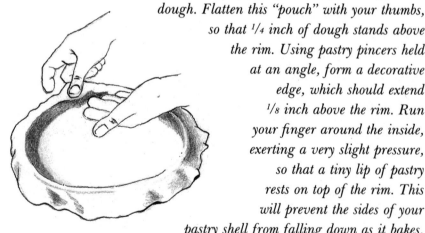

the tip of a sharp knife without removing from oven. Let tart shell cool slightly before removing ring. You may have to practice a couple of times before you get the technique right, but it is a skill worth having.

Obviously, this method is impractical if you are using a fluted quiche pan with a loose base, but you can bake a "blind," or unfilled, shell in one of these too. Simply press the dough firmly against the sides, exerting enough pressure to extend it slightly above and a fraction over the fluted rim. Prick bottom and freeze for 10 minutes. Transfer to a hot oven and check after 5 minutes. If necessary, quickly deflate any air bubbles in the pastry with the tip of a long, sharp knife. The little holes will seal themselves.

You will find that some tart recipes call for a "half-baked" pastry shell. Follow the above procedure, but bake shell for only 10 minutes, until very lightly colored.

Index:

. . . ◇ . . .

Sugar Doughs
(Pâte Brisée)
& Tarts

LEMONS
Lemon Custard Tart

LIMES
Lime Meringue Tart

MIXED FRUITS
Tarte Exotique

ORANGES
Orange Tart

PEARS
Pear and Almond Pastry Cream Tart
Tarte Berichonne (Pear Tart with Black Pepper)
Pear Soufflé Tart with Caramel Sauce

PECANS
Pecan and Hazelnut Tart

PLUMS
Santa Rosa Tart

PRUNES
Tarte Pellier

RASPBERRIES
Framboisine (Raspberry Almond Tart)
Raspberry Custard Tart

STRAWBERRIES
Strawberry Custard Tart
Napa Valley Tart

PÂTE À TARTE

(Tart Dough)

· · ·

EASY

2 eggs, large
1 tablespoon water
4 ounces (½ cup) sugar
4 ounces (1 stick) lightly salted butter, at room temperature
9 ounces (1¾ cups) all-purpose flour

Combine eggs, water, and sugar in bowl of electric mixer and mix with paddle. Add soft butter and beat in at low speed. Pour flour around edge of bowl and quickly incorporate. Dough will be soft. Gather into a ball, enclose in plastic wrap, and chill for at least 1 hour.

Butter a 9-inch pastry ring. Line a baking sheet with baking parchment and place the ring on it. On a lightly floured surface, roll dough ⅛ inch thick. Work it into a circle about 3 inches larger than your ring, rotating the dough frequently and dusting lightly with flour to make sure it doesn't stick. Line pastry ring (or fluted tart/quiche pan with loose bottom), using the technique explained on page 20, which is the same whether you bake the shell filled or unfilled. Chill pastry shell while preparing filling. *Makes one 9-inch pastry shell.*

· · · ◊ · · ·

PÂTE SUCRÉE

(Sugar Dough)

· · ·

EASY

2 eggs, large
1 tablespoon lemon juice
5 ounces (²/₃ cup), generous sugar
6 ounces (1½ sticks) lightly salted butter, at room temperature
9 ounces (1¾ cups) all-purpose flour

Combine eggs, lemon juice, and sugar in bowl of electric mixer and mix with paddle. Add soft butter and beat in at low speed. Pour flour around edge of bowl and quickly incorporate. Dough will be soft. Gather into a ball, enclose in plastic wrap, and chill for at least 1 hour.

Butter a 9-inch pastry ring. Line a baking sheet with baking parchment and place the ring on it. On a lightly floured surface, roll dough ⅛ inch thick. Work it into a circle about 3 inches larger than your ring, rotating the dough frequently and dusting lightly with flour to make sure it doesn't stick. Line pastry ring (or fluted tart/quiche pan with loose bottom), using the technique explained on page 20, which is the same whether you bake the shell filled or unfilled. Chill the pastry shell while preparing filling. *Makes one 9-inch pastry shell.*

· · · ◇ · · ·

PÂTE SUCRÉE
AUX AMANDES
(Almond Sugar Dough)

. . .

E A S Y

2 eggs, large
1 tablespoon lemon juice
4 ounces (½ cup) sugar
3½ ounces (1¾ cups) almond meal
4 ounces (1 stick) lightly salted butter, at room temperature
6 ounces (1¼ cups), scant all-purpose flour

Combine eggs, lemon juice, sugar, and almond meal in bowl of electric mixer and mix with paddle at low speed. Add soft butter and beat in at low speed until smooth. Pour flour around edge of bowl and quickly incorporate. Dough will be soft. Gather into a ball, enclose in plastic wrap, and chill for at least 1 hour.

Butter a 9-inch pastry ring. Line a baking sheet with baking parchment and place the ring on it. On a lightly floured surface, roll dough ⅛ inch thick. Work it into a circle about 3 inches larger than your ring, rotating the dough frequently and dusting lightly with flour to make sure it doesn't stick. Line pastry ring (or fluted tart/quiche pan with loose bottom), using the technique explained on page 20, which is the same whether you bake the shell filled or unfilled. Chill the pastry shell while preparing filling. *Makes one 9-inch pastry shell.*

. . . ◇ . . .

FOOD PROCESSOR
PÂTE BRISÉE
(Quick Tart Dough)

. . .

V E R Y   E A S Y

This dough is prepared in 2 minutes and gives excellent results. I do not normally recommend rolling dough out between sheets of plastic wrap, as you will not develop a "feel" for pastry this way, but in this particular case you should do so, as it is difficult to roll otherwise.

9 ounces (1¾ cups) all-purpose flour
2 tablespoons sugar
6 ounces (1½ sticks) lightly salted butter, chilled, cut in cubes
3 tablespoons cold water

Place flour, sugar, and butter in bowl of food processor fitted with steel blade. Process briefly to mix. With motor running, add water through feed tube, pulsing the machine on and off until mixture forms into large crumbs and starts to stick together. (If this doesn't happen, add a few drops of water, but too much liquid will make the dough elastic and tough.) Gather into a ball, enclose in plastic wrap, and refrigerate for 10 minutes.

Butter a 9-inch tart/quiche pan with removable bottom. Place dough between two sheets of plastic wrap. Roll out ⅛ inch thick, forming a 12-inch circle. Peel off top layer of plastic wrap and reverse dough into the pan. Quickly pull off remaining layer of plastic wrap and push dough against the fluted sides. To remove excess dough, run rolling pin across pan; the sides will act as a cutter. Place tart shell in freezer for 10 minutes before baking. *Makes one 9-inch pastry shell.*

. . . ◇ . . .

APPLE TART

Traditional French Style

. . .

INTERMEDIATE

I generally use Golden Delicious apples when making apple tarts here in California; they have a good flavor and texture and hold their shape well. The secret to getting even apple slices is to core the halved, peeled apples with a melon baller; then cut crossways. Use the short end slices for filling, where they don't show.

Pastry:

one 9-inch Pâte à Tarte shell (recipe, page 24), unbaked

Filling:

5 or 6 (2 pounds total)
  Golden Delicious apples
5 tablespoons lightly
  salted butter
5 tablespoons sugar
confectioners' sugar

Preheat oven to 400°F. Peel apples and cut in half. Remove cores with a melon baller and cut out stalks with a knife. Cut 3 apple halves into ½-inch dice and cut the remainder crossways into ⅛-inch slices.

Melt 4 tablespoons of the butter in a skillet and add the diced apples. Sprinkle with 4 tablespoons of the sugar and sauté for 5 to 8 minutes until apple cubes start to caramelize. Let cool and spoon into the prepared and chilled pastry shell. Place a circle of overlapping apple slices around the edge of the tart. Fill in the center with a few apple slices to make the surface even. Top with a second circle of apple slices, reversing the direction, making a higher center rosette. Melt remaining butter with remaining sugar and brush over tart. Dust with confectioners' sugar to promote browning. Bake for 40 to 45 minutes, until crust is golden brown and apples have started to color on top. Serve warm. *Serves 8.*

. . . ◊ . . .

A P P L E - A L M O N D   T A R T
W I T H   R A I S I N S
. . .

E A S Y

This exceptionally good tart can be prepared in just a few minutes using a food processor. Use the machine to prepare the pastry shell and process the almond filling. Sauté the apples while the pastry shell is chilling.

Pastry:

one 9-inch Pâte Brisée shell (recipe, page 27), unbaked

Filling:

1 ounce (¼ cup) seedless dark raisins
1 tablespoon dark rum
3 (1 pound total) Golden Delicious apples
1 ounce (¼ stick) unsalted butter
2 tablespoons sugar

Topping:

1 pound (2 cups) Almond Pastry Cream filling (recipe, page 110)
confectioners' sugar
4 ounces (½ cup) apricot jam for glaze (optional)

Soak raisins in rum for 15 minutes. Peel and halve apples. Remove cores with a melon baller or teaspoon and cut out stalks with a knife. Cut two apple halves crossways into ⅛-inch slices for top of tart and dice the remainder. Heat 1 tablespoon of the butter in a large skillet. Add apple slices in one layer and sprinkle with ½ tablespoon of the sugar. Allow to brown slightly on both sides, about 3 minutes, being careful to keep the slices intact. Transfer to a plate. Add remaining butter and sugar to skillet and sauté diced apples for 5 to 8 minutes over medium-high heat, until they start to caramelize. Add raisins and rum (which will evaporate) and remove from heat. Spread apple filling out on a plate and let cool.

Preheat oven to 400°F. Spread diced apples and raisins in bottom of prepared tart shell. Cover with Almond Pastry Cream filling, smoothing the top. Arrange reserved apple slices in a rose pattern in center. Dust with confectioners' sugar to promote browning and bake for 30 minutes. Crust should be golden brown and filling well baked, and the apple rosette should be tinged brown at the edges. To make glaze, heat apricot jam and then sieve. Brush lightly over top of tart. Let cool in pan on a rack. Serve at room temperature. *Serves 8.*

N O T E : Unlike most tarts, this one will hold quite well for two days.

· · · ◇ · · ·

TARTE CHIBOUSTE

. . .

Pastry:

one 9-inch Pâte Sucrée shell (recipe, page 25), unbaked

Filling:

8 ounces (1 cup) Confectioners' Custard (recipe, page 95)
2 (10 ounces total) Golden Delicious apples
2 tablespoons unsalted butter
2 tablespoons sugar
½ tablespoon Kirsch

Topping:

3 cups Crème Chibouste (recipe, page 98), flavored with Kirsch
instead of rum
confectioners' sugar

Preheat oven to 400°F. Spread Confectioners' Custard in tart shell
and bake for 25 minutes, until crust is golden.

Peel, core, and dice apples. Melt butter in a skillet, add apples,
and sprinkle with the sugar. Sauté over medium-high heat for about
7 minutes, until apples start to brown and caramelize. Sprinkle with
Kirsch, spoon over tart, and let cool.

Remove pastry ring and replace with a 9-inch cake ring, or rim
from a springform pan. Spread Crème Chibouste over tart, filling to
top of ring. Level top and chill tart for 1 hour. Run a knife blade
around sides of tart, remove ring, and dust with confectioners' sugar.
Caramelize the sugar with a hot salamander (see page 11) or slide
the tart under a preheated broiler *very briefly* until the sugar turns a
dappled golden brown. *Serves 8.*

. . . ◊ . . .

....

TARTE NORMANDE

. . .

INTERMEDIATE

This tart comes from Normandy, a region famous for its apples and apple brandy, or Calvados.

Pastry:

one 9-inch Pâte Sucrée shell (recipe, page 25), unbaked

Filling:

10 ounces (1¼ cups) Confectioners' Custard (recipe, page 95), at room temperature
1 tablespoon Calvados
2 medium (8 ounces total) Golden Delicious apples
1 ounce (¼ stick) unsalted butter
2 tablespoons sugar

Topping:

2 ounces (¼ cup), generous sugar
1 ounce (¼ cup) all-purpose flour
1 egg, large
1 tablespoon milk

Preheat oven to 400°F. Prepare pastry shell and chill while preparing the filling.

Place Confectioners' Custard in a bowl and beat in Calvados. Set aside. Peel and core apples. Cut a few thin slices for the top of the tart and reserve. Chop remaining apples into ½-inch dice. Heat butter in a skillet and add diced apples. Sprinkle with sugar and sauté over medium-low heat until golden, about 7 minutes. Mix with reserved custard and spoon into prepared pastry shell.

In a bowl, combine sugar and flour. Add egg and beat well. Add milk last and beat until mixture is smooth. Spread over apple-custard mixture. Arrange the reserved apple slices in a pinwheel on top of the tart and bake for 30 minutes, until crust is golden. Serve warm. *Serves 8.*

. . . ◇ . . .

TARTE TATIN

. . .

INTERMEDIATE

One hundred sixty-five kilometers from Paris, in the Sologne, is a little town called Lamotte-Beuvron. There, in a century-old hotel that is still in operation today, opposite the railroad station, the Demoiselles Tatin created their famous upside-down apple tart. The sisters never divulged their recipe, but I believe that my version of this rustic tart is fairly close to the original. I make it in an old and battered cake pan kept just for the purpose, but you could also use a small iron skillet. Use either Pâte Sucrée or puff paste for the pastry layer.

Pastry:

Make Pâte Sucrée (recipe, page 25) and roll dough out ¼ inch thick.

Filling:

3 tablespoons unsalted butter
2 tablespoons sugar
3 (1 pound total) Golden Delicious apples

Preheat oven to 400°F. Grease an 8-inch heavy cake pan or iron skillet with half the butter and sprinkle with the sugar. Peel and core apples and cut into sixths. In a separate skillet, melt remaining butter and sauté apples over high heat for about 7 minutes, until they start to

....

color but do not give up their juices. Arrange apples in the prepared pan, packing the pieces close together. Top with an 8-inch circle of Pâte Sucrée, ¼ inch thick, which goes *inside* the pan. Pat dough down over the apples—it will look lumpy—and make several slits for steam to escape. Bake for 50 minutes, covering the top loosely with a sheet of foil after 30 minutes so that the pastry does not burn. Let cool for 10 minutes. Place pan over high heat for 7 minutes to caramelize surface of apples to a deep, golden brown. Hold a plate over the pan and reverse to unmold tart. If a couple of pieces of apple remain stuck, which often happens, just pick them up with a knife and return them where they belong. Serve tart immediately. *Serves 8.*

· · · ◊ · · ·

A P R I C O T   T A R T

Traditional French Style

· · ·

E A S Y

Fresh apricots often taste disappointingly bland, but develop acidity and a very pleasing flavor when cooked. You can use a Pâte à Tarte or puff paste (recipe, page 24) for this dessert; both kinds are delicious.

Pastry:

one 9″ Pâte à Tarte shell (recipe, page 24), unbaked

Filling:

1 pound (about 20) firm ripe apricots
1 pint (2 cups) Simple Syrup (recipe, page 237)
6 ounces (¾ cup) Almond Pastry Cream filling (recipe, page 110)
confectioner's sugar
4 ounces (½ cup) Apricot Glaze (recipe, page 241)

Make a circular cut around each apricot, slicing through to the pit. Twist the two halves to separate. Lift out pit, which will remain attached to one half. Bring syrup to a boil, add apricots, and simmer gently for 5 minutes. Drain well, reserving syrup for another use. (It will keep for several days under refrigeration.)

Preheat oven to 400°F. Spread prepared, chilled pastry shell with almond filling. Push apricots into the filling at a slight angle, cut side up. Dust with confectioners' sugar to help browning. Bake for 30 minutes until crust is golden brown. Brush tart with warm apricot glaze and serve warm or cold with Crème Anglaise (recipe, page 100) flavored with Cointreau. *Serves 8.*

· · · ◊ · · ·

WARM BANANA TART

. . .

This is a very easy tart to prepare ahead and assemble at the last minute: a baked tart shell is filled with rum-flavored Confectioners' Custard, topped with sliced bananas, and heated for 5 minutes.

Pastry:

one 9-inch Pâte Sucrée shell (recipe, page 25) or Pâte Brisée shell (recipe, page 27), fully baked

Filling:

10 ounces (1¼ cups) Confectioners' Custard (recipe, page 95), at room temperature
1 tablespoon dark rum
2 ounces (½ stick) unsalted butter, soft
2 or 3 bananas
2 tablespoons lemon juice

Preheat oven to 400°F. Prepare and bake pastry shell and set aside. Place Confectioners' Custard in a bowl and add rum. Beat in butter little by little to make a smooth emulsion. Spread custard into baked and cooled shell, which can remain in the pastry ring. Slice bananas thinly at a slight angle and arrange in overlapping circles on top of the custard, reversing the direction of each smaller circle. Brush lightly with lemon juice, without disturbing the position of the banana slices. Transfer tart to oven and bake for 5 minutes. Serve warm. *Serves 8.*

. . . ◊ . . .

BLUEBERRY MACAROON TART

. . .

Pastry:

one 9-inch Pâte Sucrée shell (recipe, page 25), unbaked

Filling:

8 ounces (1 cup) Confectioners' Custard (recipe, page 95)
6 ounces (1 cup) fresh blueberries
2 tablespoons English gin
1 ounce (¼ stick) unsalted butter
2 egg whites, large
2 ounces (¼ cup) sugar
2 ounces (½ cup) almond meal (page 1)
1 whole egg, large
2 ounces (½ cup), scant all-purpose flour
1 ounce (¼ cup) sliced almonds
confectioners' sugar

Preheat oven to 375°F. Spoon custard into the chilled, unbaked pastry shell. Cover custard with blueberries and sprinkle with gin.

In a small saucepan, melt butter and allow to brown slightly. Let cool to lukewarm. Whip the egg whites to stiff peaks. Combine sugar with the almond meal. In a separate bowl, beat the whole egg and add the sugar-almond mixture. Pour in the butter and beat in the flour. Loosen the mixture with a little of the whipped egg whites, then fold in the remainder. Spread an even layer of macaroon mixture on top of tart (but not over the pastry edge) and sprinkle with sliced almonds. Dust with confectioners' sugar to help browning. Bake for 30 to 35 minutes, until crust is golden. Dust with additional confectioners' sugar and serve warm. *Serves 8.*

COUNTRY-STYLE
CHERRY TART

. . .

EASY

Pastry:

one 9-inch Pâte à Tarte shell (recipe, page 24) or Pâte Brisée
shell (recipe, page 27), unbaked

Filling:

1 pound (4 cups) ripe cherries, such as Bing or Queen Anne
5 ounces (½ cup), generous Confectioners' Custard (recipe, page
  95)
2 tablespoons Kirsch
1 tablespoon Simple Syrup (recipe, page 237)

Preheat oven to 400°F. Wash, stem, and pit the cherries. Stir 1 tablespoon of the Kirsch into the custard. Spread pastry shell with
custard and top with cherries, arranging them as close together as
possible. Bake for 20 to 25 minutes until crust is golden brown.
Combine Simple Syrup and remaining Kirsch in a small saucepan,
heat to lukewarm, and carefully set alight. Pour flaming Kirsch over
tart. Serve at room temperature. *Serves 8.*

. . . ◇ . . .

C L A F O U T I S

. . .

E A S Y

This famous dessert was originally a specialty of the Auvergne, and consisted of cherries (often unpitted!) baked in a batter—in short, a good old French country dish. I make a lighter version, not unlike an extra-deep quiche with a cherry-studded custard, and bake it in a cake pan.

Pastry:

Follow directions for Pâte Sucrée (recipe, page 25).

Filling:

1 pint (2 cups) milk
6 eggs, large
6 ounces (¾ cup), scant sugar with a dash of vanilla
1 pound (4 cups) ripe cherries, such as Bing or
    Queen Anne, pitted

Preheat oven to 375°F. Grease a 9-inch cake pan liberally with butter. Roll pastry out ⅛ inch thick and line pan, being careful to fit dough against the sides without stretching it. Run a rolling pin across the top of the pan to cut off excess pastry.

In a bowl, combine milk, eggs, and sugar and beat until well mixed. Arrange cherries in pastry shell and pour custard mixture over them. (A few of the cherries will float.) Bake for 45 minutes, or until crust is golden and the filling is dappled brown on top. Serve warm. *Serves 8.*

. . . ◊ . . .

LEMON CUSTARD TART

. . .

INTERMEDIATE

Pastry:

one 9-inch Pâte Sucrée shell (recipe, page 25), half-baked

Filling:

8 ounces (1 cup) Confectioners' Custard (recipe, page 95)
at room temperature
2 or 3 lemons
5 ounces (⅔ cup), scant sugar
5 eggs, large
3 ounces (¾ stick) unsalted butter, soft

Preheat oven to 385°F. Spread custard in the half-baked pastry shell.
Bake for 20 to 25 minutes, until crust is golden.

In the meantime, peel one of the lemons with a vegetable peeler,
shaving off only the zest or colored part. Chop fine. Squeeze lemons
and measure out 5 ounces of the juice. Reserve 1 teaspoon of the
lemon zest for decoration and place the remainder with the lemon
juice in a non-aluminum saucepan. Add sugar and eggs and beat
well. Whisk vigorously over moderate heat until mixture thickens, at
165°F. (Be careful not to boil, or eggs will turn grainy.) Remove from
heat and beat in butter a little at a time. Pour over baked tart and
bake for 5 minutes at 385°F. Let cool and sprinkle center area with
reserved lemon zest. Serve at room temperature. *Serves 8.*

VARIATION: To make an Orange Tart, substitute orange zest and
orange juice for the lemon zest and lemon juice.

. . . ◊ . . .

LIME MERINGUE TART

. . .

Pastry:

one 9-inch Pâte Sucrée shell (recipe, page 25), unbaked

Filling:

8 ounces (1 cup) Confectioners' Custard (recipe, page 95),
  at room temperature
3 or 4 limes
5 eggs, large
3 ounces (¾ stick) unsalted butter, soft

Topping:

2 egg whites, large
4 ounces (½ cup) sugar
2 tablespoons water

Preheat oven to 385°F. Spread custard in pastry shell. Bake for 20
to 25 minutes, until crust is golden and custard is dappled brown on
top.

In the meantime, peel 2 of the limes with a vegetable peeler, shaving off only the zest or colored part. Chop fine. Squeeze limes and
measure out 5 ounces of the strained juice. Reserve 1 teaspoon of
the lime zest for decoration and place the remainder with the lime
juice in a non-aluminum saucepan. Add eggs and beat well. Whisk
vigorously over moderate heat until custard mixture thickens, at 165°F.
(Be careful not to boil, or the eggs will turn grainy.) Remove from
heat and beat in butter a little at a time.

Beat egg whites until stiff. Place the sugar in a saucepan (preferably
of unlined copper) with water and boil to 230°F. or soft ball. Pour
over egg whites in a thin stream, whisking hard at the same time.
Fold into the warm lime filling. Pile the meringue mixture over baked

tart. Bake for 10 to 15 minutes at 385°F. until golden on top. Let cool and sprinkle center area with reserved lime zest. Serve at room temperature. *Serves 8.*

· · · ◇ · · ·

TARTE EXOTIQUE
· · ·
INTERMEDIATE

This glittering, very impressive dessert is nothing more than a pastry shell filled with almond pastry filling that is baked and then soaked with Kirsch syrup. Brilliantly colored fruits, some of them tropical, are arranged on top, and the tart is then glazed.

Pastry:

one 9-inch Pâte Sucrée shell (recipe, page 25), unbaked

Filling:

4 ounces (½ cup) raspberry jam
12 ounces (1½ cups) Almond Pastry Cream filling (recipe, page 110)

Syrup:

2 tablespoons Simple Syrup (recipe, page 237)
2 tablespoons Kirsch

Topping:

fresh raspberries
ripe strawberries
seedless (or seeded) grapes

½ ripe mango
1 ripe kiwi
1 ripe litchi
4 ounces (½ cup) Apricot Glaze (recipe, page 241)

Preheat oven to 385°F. Spread the unbaked pastry shell with raspberry jam and top with the almond filling. Bake for 25 minutes, until
crust is golden. Let cool.

Mix Simple Syrup and Kirsch together and brush over tart. Peel
and slice fruits as necessary and arrange close together on top of tart
(see illustration) in an asymmetrical pattern. Brush with hot Apricot
Glaze. Serve at room temperature. *Serves 8.*

· · · ◇ · · ·

PEAR AND ALMOND
PASTRY CREAM TART

. . .

INTERMEDIATE

Pastry:

one 9-inch Pâte Sucrée (recipe, page 25) or Pâte Brisée shell (recipe, page 27), unbaked

Filling:

5 medium (1½ pounds) ripe, firm pears, such as Bartletts or Bosc
1 pint (2 cups) Simple Syrup (recipe, page 237)
8 ounces (1 cup) Almond Pastry Cream filling (recipe, page 110)
4 ounces (½ cup) Apricot Glaze (recipe, page 241)

Maple Caramel Sauce:

8 ounces (1 cup) pure maple syrup
1 tablespoon dark rum
4 ounces (½ cup) heavy cream

Peel and halve pears. Remove cores with a melon baller or teaspoon and cut out stems. In a large saucepan, bring Simple Syrup to a boil. Add pears and poach gently for 5 minutes. Drain, and set one pear half aside. (Reserve syrup for another use; it will keep under refrigeration for several days.) Cut remaining pear halves across into ½-inch slices, keeping slices together. Trim the reserved pear half into a round shape for center of tart.

Preheat oven to 400°F. Spread pastry shell with Almond Pastry Cream filling. Pick up each sliced pear half on a spatula and place on top of tart, with stem ends pointing toward the center. Fan the slices out slightly. Place rounded pear in center. Bake tart for 30 to 40 minutes, until crust is golden brown. Brush with hot Apricot Glaze. Serve warm with Maple Caramel Sauce. *Serves 8.*

. . . .

TO MAKE SAUCE: Put maple syrup in a heavy pan, bring to a boil, and reduce slightly over high heat, about 5 minutes. Stir in rum and cream. Let simmer for 1 minute, stirring, and transfer to sauceboat. *Serve warm.*

. . . ◊ . . .

TARTE BERICHONNE
(Pear Tart with Black Pepper)

. . .

V E R Y   E A S Y

In France, I use William pears when preparing this tart; in California, I use Bartletts. The addition of ground black pepper may sound bizarre, but I assure you that it brings out the flavor of the pears magnificently.

Pastry:

one 9-inch Pâte Brisée shell (recipe, page 27), unbaked, chilled

Filling:

2 to 3 (10 ounces total) firm, ripe Bartlett pears
1 tablespoon Kirsch
freshly ground black pepper
8 ounces (1 cup) Almond Pastry Cream filling (recipe, page 110)
confectioners' sugar

Preheat oven to 375°F. Peel, core, and dice pears. Spread evenly on bottom of prepared, chilled pastry shell. Sprinkle with the Kirsch and a generous grinding of black pepper. Top with Almond Pastry Cream, smoothing the top. Bake tart for 30 to 35 minutes until crust is golden brown. Dust lightly with confectioners' sugar. Serve warm or at room temperature. *Serves 8.*

N O T E : This tart will hold quite well for two days.

PEAR SOUFFLÉ TART
WITH CARAMEL SAUCE

. . .

Pastry:

one 9-inch Pâte Sucrée shell (recipe, page 25), unbaked, chilled

Filling:

8 ounces (1 cup) Confectioners' Custard (recipe, page 95), cooled
2 medium (10 ounces total) firm, ripe Bartlett pears
1 pint (2 cups) Heavy Syrup (recipe, page 238)
2 tablespoons Kirsch

Topping:

½ ounce (2 envelopes) unflavored gelatin
4 tablespoons water
5 egg yolks, large
2 ounces (½ cup), scant all-purpose flour
10 ounces (1¼ cups) sugar
6 ounces (¾ cup) milk, boiling
5 egg whites, large

Caramel Sauce:

8 ounces (1 cup) sugar
3 tablespoons water
2 ounces (½ stick) unsalted butter
4 ounces (½ cup) heavy cream

Preheat oven to 375°F. Spread uncooked, chilled tart shell with custard and bake for 20 minutes. In the meantime, peel, halve, and core
pears. Bring syrup to the boil, add pears, and simmer gently for 5
minutes. Drain, and cut into dice. (Save syrup for another use; it will

. . . .

keep in the refrigerator for several days.) Spoon fruit evenly over custard and sprinkle with the Kirsch.

TOPPING: Dissolve gelatin in 2 tablespoons water. Beat egg yolks until light and fluffy. Add flour and 2 ounces of the sugar to egg yolks, mix well, and pour boiling milk on top. Return combined mixture to pan, add gelatin, and stir briskly until custard boils, thickens, and turns "shiny." Remove from heat.

Beat egg whites until stiff. Put remaining 6 ounces sugar in a saucepan, preferably of unlined copper, with 2 tablespoons water and boil to 230°F., or soft ball stage. Pour in a thin stream over egg whites, beating vigorously at the same time. Fold this meringue mixture into the custard.

Line a baking sheet with baking parchment and set the filled tart on it. Carefully place a 9-inch cake ring or the rim from a springform pan over the tart. Cover with custard-meringue mixture until level with top of ring. Bake tart for 15 to 20 minutes, until golden. Run a knife around edge and remove ring. Serve hot with Caramel Sauce. *Serves 8.*

CARAMEL SAUCE: Combine sugar with water in a saucepan, preferably of unlined copper. Boil until syrup becomes a dark golden caramel color; watch it carefully (350°F. on candy thermometer). Off the heat, stir in the butter and the cream, adding more cream if the sauce is too thick to pour. Serve warm with the hot tart.

· · · ◇ · · ·

PECAN AND
HAZELNUT TART

. . .

INTERMEDIATE

Pastry:

one 9-inch Pâte Sucrée shell (recipe, page 25) or Pâte Brisée shell (recipe, page 27), baked and cooled

Filling:

4 ounces (⅔ cup) hazelnuts
8 ounces (1¾ cups) pecan halves
2 tablespoons milk
2 ounces semisweet chocolate
2 tablespoons golden raisins
8 ounces (1 cup) pure maple syrup
4 ounces (½ cup) heavy cream
½ tablespoon unsalted butter

Preheat oven to 350°F. Place hazelnuts on a baking sheet and bake for 10 minutes, until lightly toasted. Wrap hot nuts in a clean kitchen towel and rub them together to remove skins. Cut each hazelnut in half and place in a bowl. Stir in pecans and set aside.

Heat milk in a small saucepan and add chocolate. Stir until melted, then pour into pastry shell and spread over bottom surface. Refrigerate until chocolate hardens, about 10 minutes. Scatter raisins in bottom of shell.

Put maple syrup in a heavy saucepan, preferably of unlined copper, and boil until the mixture reduces and caramelizes, at 350°F. on a candy thermometer. Stir in cream and butter and let boil for 2 minutes. Pour over nuts and mix well. Spread combined mixture into prepared tart shell. Serve tart at room temperature. *Serves 8.*

NOTE: The nuts should be coated with a thin, shiny layer of cara-melized maple syrup, which sticks them together as it hardens. If your nut and sauce mixture is too liquid, simply pour it into a large sauté pan and reduce over high heat until the liquid has almost evaporated. The filling will probably be dull rather than shiny but will taste fine.

$$\cdots \diamond \cdots$$

SANTA ROSA TART

. . .

VERY EASY

As with many traditional French country-style tarts, this one is memorable when served warm from the oven, and not at all successful a few hours later, as the fruit inevitably softens the pastry. I like to use Santa Rosa plums in California, but any sweet, ripe plums will give you good results.

Pastry:

one 9-inch Pâte Brisée shell (recipe, page 27), unbaked

Filling:

2 pounds ripe Santa Rosa plums, unpeeled
1 pint (2 cups) Simple Syrup (recipe, page 237)
1 tablespoon sugar
1 tablespoon Cognac

Preheat oven to 400°F. Prepare pastry shell. Make a circular cut around each plum, slicing through to the pit. Twist the two halves to separate. Remove pit, which will remain attached to one half, either lifting or cutting it out depending on the variety of fruit. (Some are freestone.) In a saucepan large enough to hold the fruit in a single layer, bring Simple Syrup to the boil. Add plums and poach gently for 5 minutes. Drain fruit, reserving the syrup for another use. (It will keep for several days under refrigeration.)

Arrange the plums cut side down on the pastry shell, pushing them as close together as possible. Sprinkle with the sugar and bake for 25 minutes until crust is golden brown. Sprinkle tart with Cognac and serve warm. *Serves 8.*

· · · ◇ · · ·

TARTE PELLIER
· · ·

INTERMEDIATE

I named this tart for Louis Pellier, the Frenchman who introduced the Prune d'Agen (a variety of plum that dries particularly well) to California back in 1856. Those first cuttings made the long sea voyage around the Horn stuck in raw potatoes, which were buried in sawdust and packed inside two leather trunks. Pellier grafted the survivors onto rootstocks of the native wild plum, and thereby started a huge industry—California supplies much of the world prune crop today.

Pastry:

Pâte Sucrée (recipe, page 25)
1 teaspoon cinnamon

Filling:

1 pound soft, pitted prunes
1 pint (2 cups) Simple Syrup (recipe, page 237)
2 egg whites, large

1 tablespoon Candied Ginger in Syrup, finely chopped
1 egg yolk, for glaze
1 tablespoon water
pinch salt

Make Pâte Sucrée according to the recipe, sifting cinnamon and flour together. Butter a 9-inch pastry ring. Line a baking sheet with baking parchment and place the ring on it. On a lightly floured surface, roll the dough into a ¼ inch thick circle. Place the dough in the ring, pushing it against the sides without stretching it. Run a rolling pin across the ring to cut off excess; the rim will act as a cutter. Chill pastry shell until required. Roll the remaining dough ⅛ inch thick for lattice top. Place on a baking sheet and refrigerate; it cuts easily when cold.

Preheat oven to 400°F. Poach prunes in syrup for 20 minutes, until very soft. Drain, and place in bowl of food processor. Add 2 tablespoons of Simple Syrup (or use syrup from candied ginger) and process until puréed. Add egg whites and finely chopped ginger and process just until blended. Spoon prune mixture into pastry shell. Cut remaining dough into narrow strips and arrange in a lattice pattern on top of filling. Make egg wash by combining egg yolk with water and a small pinch of salt, which promotes a better color and shine. Brush egg wash over tart. Bake for 25 minutes, until pastry is golden brown. Serve at room temperature. *Serves 8.*

· · · ◊ · · ·

F R A M B O I S I N E

(Raspberry Almond Tart)

. . .

Pastry:

one 9-inch Pâte Sucrée shell (recipe, page 25), unbaked

Filling:

4 ounces (½ cup) fresh raspberries
2 ounces (¼ cup) sugar
or
6 ounces (¾ cup) best-quality raspberry jam

Topping:

5 egg whites, large
pinch salt
1 ounce (¼ stick) unsalted butter
3 ounces (¾ cup) almond meal
3 ounces (⅓ cup) generous sugar
1 ounce (¼ cup) flour
2 tablespoons sliced almonds
confectioners' sugar

Preheat oven to 400°F. Crush raspberries and sugar together lightly and spread in pastry shell. (Or substitute jam.)

Place 4 of the egg whites in bowl of electric mixer, add salt, and beat to stiff peaks. Melt butter and allow to brown slightly. Cool to lukewarm. In a separate bowl, combine almond meal, sugar, remaining egg white and melted butter. Working very quickly, loosen this mixture with a little of the beaten egg white. Lightly fold in the remaining egg whites and the flour. It is important to do this fast, or the mixture will deflate. Immediately pour mixture over raspberries. Top with sliced almonds and dust with confectioners' sugar. Bake for 25 minutes, until soft macaroon topping and pastry crust are golden. Serve at room temperature. *Serves 8.*

STRAWBERRY
CUSTARD TART

. . .

INTERMEDIATE

Pastry:

one 9-inch Pâte Sucrée aux Amandes shell (recipe, page 26), fully baked and cooled

Filling:

8 ounces (1 cup) Confectioners' Custard (recipe, page 95) at room temperature
½ tablespoon Kirsch
4 ounces (1 stick) unsalted butter, soft
2 pounds (3 baskets) ripe strawberries, medium size
8 ounces (1 cup) strawberry jelly, melted

Stir Kirsch into Confectioners' Custard and beat in butter, little by little, to make a smooth emulsion. Spread in pastry shell. Wash, dry, and hull berries. Slice in half and lay in overlapping circles on custard filling, reversing the direction of each row. Put one whole berry in center. Brush with melted strawberry jelly and refrigerate. Serve within 8 hours for the best texture. *Serves 8.*

VARIATION: To make a Raspberry Custard Tart, substitute fresh raspberries and raspberry jelly for the strawberries and strawberry jelly.

. . . ◊ . . .

NAPA VALLEY TART
. . .

This tart has a top layer of strawberries in wine gelatin, which contrasts beautifully with the almond filling and crisp pastry. The gelatin sets up separately in an ordinary disposable aluminum foil pie pan—be sure that it is the same diameter as your tart.

Pastry:

one 9-inch Pâte Sucrée shell (recipe, page 25), unbaked, chilled

Filling:

8 ounces (1 cup) Almond Pastry Cream filling (recipe, page 110)
2 tablespoons Simple Syrup (recipe, page 237)
1 pint (2 cups) red wine, preferably Napa Valley Cabernet
   Sauvignon
½ ounce (2 envelopes) unflavored gelatin
2 tablespoons cold water
2 ounces (¼ cup) sugar
12 ounces (1 basket) ripe strawberries

Preheat oven to 400°F. Spread chilled, unbaked tart shell with almond pastry filling. Bake for 25 minutes, until crust is golden. Let cool. Combine syrup and 2 tablespoons of the wine and brush over tart.
   Soak the gelatin in cold water for 5 minutes. Heat 1 cup of the wine and stir in gelatin and sugar, making sure both are completely dissolved. Remove from heat and stir in the remaining cup of wine. Let stand until cool but do not allow to set. Pour a thin layer of gelatin in the bottom of a 9-inch aluminum pie pan and chill for 10 minutes, until set. Hull and halve strawberries. Arrange in pie pan and carefully pour remaining wine gelatin on top. Refrigerate until set, about 1 hour. Unmold upside down on top of tart and serve immediately. *Serves 8.*

2.

Cream Puff Doughs (Pâte à Choux) & Uses

· · · ◇ · · ·

Unlike other pastry doughs, this one is partly cooked before forming and baking. It is made by bringing butter and water to a boil, then adding flour all at once and stirring vigorously for a few minutes to evaporate excess moisture. The paste is then cooled slightly, and eggs are beaten in one at a time. I like to have a soft dough that falls from a spatula in a soft ribbon—it bakes into a pastry that is crisp on the outside and tender within, and melts in the mouth. Incidentally, good choux pastry is meant to be crisp on the outside and have a soft center with lots of holes. It is not supposed to be hard, brittle, or hollow on the inside.

The same basic paste is used for a number of classic pastries, including éclairs, puffs, Paris-Brest, and Gâteau Saint Honoré. Choux puffs can be filled with savory mixtures, in which case the sugar is omitted from the dough. A crisp, unfilled Burgundian pâte à choux specialty, Gougère, includes cheese—see recipe, page 62. It makes a delicious hot appetizer with a glass of wine.

Index:

· · · ◊ · · ·

Cream Puff Doughs (Pâte à Choux) & Uses

Pâte à Choux
Éclairs
Puffs
Croquettes

Paris-Brest (Cream Puff Ring)
Gâteau Saint Honoré
Gougère

PÂTE À CHOUX

. . .

8 ounces (1 cup) water
pinch salt
1 teaspoon sugar
4 ounces (1 stick) unsalted butter, cut up
5 ounces (1 cup), scant all-purpose flour
5 eggs, large

Preheat oven to 400°F. Line a baking sheet with baking parchment and fit a pastry bag with a plain ½-inch round tube.

Combine water, salt, sugar, and butter in a heavy saucepan. Bring to a boil and add flour all at once. Stir vigorously for 2 minutes over medium heat until well amalgamated and mixture pulls away from side of pan. Transfer to bowl of electric mixer and beat for 3 to 4 minutes at low speed to cool mixture. Add eggs one at a time, making sure each is incorporated before adding the next one. Beat at medium-high speed until mixture is smooth and shiny. Transfer to pastry bag and pipe into desired shapes (see next page). Bake for 20 minutes or until well puffed and golden. *Makes approximately 2½ cups of choux paste.*

. . . ◊ . . .

ÉCLAIRS, PUFFS,
AND CROQUETTES
. . .

INTERMEDIATE

1¼ cups Pâte à Choux paste (recipe, page 57)
2 cups pastry cream (recipe, page 95)
fondant icing (recipe, page 239)
confectioners' sugar
coarse granulated sugar

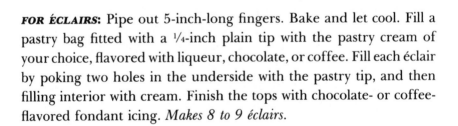

FOR ÉCLAIRS: Pipe out 5-inch-long fingers. Bake and let cool. Fill a pastry bag fitted with a ¼-inch plain tip with the pastry cream of your choice, flavored with liqueur, chocolate, or coffee. Fill each éclair by poking two holes in the underside with the pastry tip, and then filling interior with cream. Finish the tops with chocolate- or coffee-flavored fondant icing. *Makes 8 to 9 éclairs.*

FOR PUFFS: Pipe out 2-inch-diameter mounds. Bake and let cool. Fit a pastry bag with a large star tip and fill puffs with the pastry cream of your choice. Slice the tops off the puffs and fill with cream. Replace tops at a slight angle, and dust with confectioners' sugar. *Makes 6 to 7 puffs.*

FOR CROQUETTES: Pipe out 1-inch-diameter swirls using a star tube. Sprinkle with coarse sugar crystals. When baked and cooled, split and fill with the pastry cream of your choice. *Makes 12 to 14 croquettes.*

PARIS-BREST

(Cream Puff Ring)

. . .

INTERMEDIATE

According to legend, this pastry was named in honor of a famous bicycle race that is held in France each year—the contestants race from Paris to Brest and back. At one time the choux ring was filled with praliné-flavored buttercream, which made it extremely rich. I think it is better filled with a lighter pastry cream, but we retain the praliné flavoring.

1¼ cups Pâte à Choux (one-half of recipe, page 57)
1 egg yolk, for glaze
1 teaspoon water
2 tablespoons sliced almonds
3½ cups Crème Liegeoise (recipe, page 96)
3 tablespoons Praliné Paste (recipe, page 248)
confectioners' sugar

Preheat oven to 400°F. and line a baking sheet with baking parchment. Make Pâte à Choux according to the recipe and, using a pastry bag fitted with a ½-inch tip, pipe out a 9-inch circle. Pipe a second circle inside the first one. The two circles of dough should touch each other. Pipe a third circle of dough on top of the first two, pyramid style. Blend egg yolk with water and brush over ring. Sprinkle top with sliced almonds and bake for 20 minutes. Reduce heat to 350°F. and continue baking for another 10 to 15 minutes, until well risen and golden. Cool on rack.

Make Crème Liegeoise, flavoring with praliné paste. Transfer to a pastry bag fitted with a large star tip. Split the Pâte à Choux ring horizontally and fill the bottom half with cream, making a decorative design, as the edges will show. Replace top and dust with confectioners' sugar. Refrigerate until serving time, which should be within 4 hours for the best texture. *Serves 8.*

....

GÂTEAU SAINT HONORÉ

. . .

This classic dessert was named in honor of Saint Honoré, the patron saint of pastry cooks, and I suppose it represents his heavenly crown. The contrast of textures and flavors is certainly out of this world! A base of flaky pastry is topped with a ring of Pâte à Choux surmounted with caramel-glazed choux puffs. The center is filled with Crème Chibouste. Use any of the puff doughs on pages 66 through 71 for the base.

½ pound puff dough of choice (recipes, pages 66 through 71)
1¼ cups Pâte à Choux (recipe, page 57)
8 ounces (1 cup) Confectioners' Custard (recipe, page 95)
3 cups Crème Chibouste (recipe, page 98)
8 ounces (1 cup) sugar, for caramel glaze
⅓ cup water

Preheat oven to 390°F. Line a baking sheet with baking parchment. Roll out puff dough ⅛ inch thick and cut out a 9½-inch circle, using a cake pan as a guide. Place on a baking sheet and chill while preparing Pâte à Choux.

Make Pâte à Choux according to the recipe. Transfer to pastry bag fitted with a ½-inch plain round tip. Pipe an even rim around the edge of the puff dough circle. Alongside, on the baking sheet, pipe out twelve 1-inch balls. Squeeze the remaining choux paste in an open spiral shape on the puff dough, inside the rim. Bake for 25 to 30 minutes, removing puffs after about 15 minutes or as soon as they are ready. Let cool on rack.

Place Confectioners' Custard in a pastry bag fitted with a ¼-inch plain round tip. Poke a little hole in the bottom of each choux puff and fill with custard. Set aside. Prepare Crème Chibouste.

Transfer pastry base to a suitable flat serving platter. Place sugar and water in a heavy pan, preferably of unlined copper, and boil to the hard crack stage, 310°F. on a candy thermometer. Remove

. . . .

60   La Nouvelle Pâtisserie

pan from heat, or the light caramel will become too thick.
Dip each filled choux puff in the caramel glaze,
holding it on the tip of a knife, and place
around the top of the ring. The puffs
should touch each other. (Do *not*
be tempted to push them in place
with your finger; the caramel is
very hot!) Using a large star tip,
fill the center of the crown with
Crème Chibouste and pipe rosettes
between the glazed puffs. Refrigerate
the Gâteau Saint Honoré until serving time,
ideally not more than 4 hours. *Serves 8.*

. . . ◊ . . .

GOUGÈRE

. . .

EASY

A specialty of Burgundy, this crisp, cheese-flavored choux ring is served warm as an accompaniment to a glass or two of full-bodied red wine. It is an excellent hors d'oeuvre, and you can also serve it with a salad for lunch.

8 ounces (1 cup) water, plus 1 tablespoon for glaze
4 ounces (1 stick) lightly salted butter
½ teaspoon salt
4 ounces (¾ cup) all-purpose flour
4 eggs, large
4 ounces Gruyère (imported Swiss) cheese, cut in ¼-inch dice
1 egg yolk, for glaze

Preheat oven to 375°F. Line a baking sheet with baking parchment.

Combine water, butter, and salt in a heavy pan. Bring to a boil and add the flour all at once. Stir vigorously for 2 minutes over medium heat until well amalgamated and mixture pulls away from sides of pan. Transfer to bowl of electric mixer and beat for 3 to 4 minutes at low speed to cool the paste. Beat in the eggs one by one, making sure that each is amalgamated before adding the next. Beat to a smooth paste. Stir in about two-thirds of the cheese. Drop adjoining spoonfuls of dough in two 8-inch-diameter circles on the prepared baking sheet. Blend the egg yolk with 1 tablespoon water and brush over rings. Dot the remaining cheese on top, pushing the cubes in lightly. Bake for about 45 minutes, until well risen, browned, and crispy. Pull apart to serve. Serve hot. *Makes two rings, sufficient for 8 persons.*

. . . ◇ . . .

3.

Puff Doughs or Flaky Pastries (Pâte Feuilletée) & Uses

. . . ◊ . . .

Classic French puff dough is the most interesting of all the basic doughs to work with, and the most impressive when well made. When made in the classic way, a flour and water paste is wrapped around a large rectangle of cold butter and then rolled and folded a set number of times to produce over seven hundred layers of butter and dough. Puff paste rises in the oven because the steam trapped in the layers forces them apart and upward.

There are several different ways to make puff paste, of which I have listed four, and I recommend that you start with the easiest, the Écossaise, or Scottish, method.

With puff paste on hand—most types keep well in the refrigerator for several days, and can be frozen if formed into the shapes in which they are to be baked—you can make a great deal out of very little from appetizers to desserts.

The puff doughs I have listed can be used interchangeably for any of the recipes that follow. When making puff paste, it is important to keep the dough cool at all times. If it becomes difficult to handle, simply return to the refrigerator until the butter firms up again. The dough must be allowed to rest in the refrigerator between "turns" or it becomes elastic and resists rolling out. I do not recommend making puff paste on a hot day, as the butter tends to melt and come through the dough.

Always chill your puff dough for at least 20 minutes after forming into the required shapes; otherwise it will shrink in the oven and rise unevenly. Then apply egg wash if used, and bake. Preformed and frozen puff paste items can go straight from the freezer to the oven.

The best surface to work on, if possible, is a marble slab, but you can make good puff dough on a countertop. You should have a straight, heavy, professional rolling pin of polished hardwood about 18 inches long. A flimsy rolling pin is not an effective tool. I use ordinary all-purpose flour and lightly salted butter—there are no "magic" ingredients. It does take practice to make really light, airy puff dough, but even a first try at the Écossaise should produce an agreeably flaky pastry. And each succeeding attempt will improve your skill.

Index:

· · · ◇ · · ·

Puff Doughs or Flaky Pastries (Pâte Feuilletée) & Uses

PUFF DOUGHS
Écossaise (Scottish) Method
Semidirect Method
Direct or Classic Method
Inversée (Butter Outside) Method

Puff Dough Tart Shells
Vol au Vent ("Puffs of Wind" or Patty Shells)
Apple Chaussons
Jam Turnovers
Cheese Twists
Allumettes (Sugar Matchsticks)
Palmiers
Bamboo
Gâteau Napoléon
Gâteau Pithiviers

PUFF DOUGH

Écossaise (Scottish) Method

. . .

INTERMEDIATE

This is called the Scottish method because it is the traditional way of making flaky pastry in Scotland—the cut-up butter is mixed with the flour and the dough is then rolled out, as opposed to wrapping a large rectangle of butter inside the dough. (Centuries ago, Catholic Scotland had strong ties with France, and this influenced the cuisine, at least in court circles. Even today there are many French words in Scottish culinary use. For example, a plate or platter, assiette *in French, is an* ashet *in Scotland.)*

1 pound 2 ounces (3¾ cups) all-purpose flour
½ ounce (2 teaspoons) salt
9 ounces (1⅛ cups) water
10 ounces (2½ sticks) lightly salted butter, cold

Place flour, salt, and water in bowl of electric mixer. Mix by hand and then, using a dough hook, mix until almost combined but not yet smooth. Cut butter into small cubes and add to bowl. Combine lightly—the pieces of butter must be evenly distributed but should not disappear. Gather the crumbly dough together and turn out onto a lightly floured surface.

Roll dough into a large rectangle, dusting lightly with flour so that it does not stick to the rolling pin or the work surface. It should be

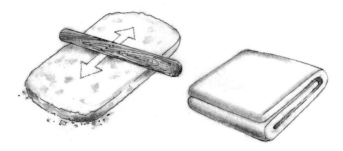

three times longer than its width and ¼ inch thick. Fold in three like a business letter and roll lightly to make level and seal together. Give a quarter turn to the left so that the fold is perpendicular to you, and dough will be rolled in the opposite direction the next time. (This equalizes tension within the dough.) Rapidly roll into a 10-by-15-inch rectangle. Be careful not to roll over the edges, or the butter will break through the dough. Keep the edges straight by pushing against dough with length of rolling pin. Repeat the folding procedure and roll lightly to seal. You have now completed two "single turns." Make two indentations in the dough with your finger, one under the other, to signify two turns. Wrap in plastic and refrigerate for 30 minutes.

Repeat the above rolling, folding, and chilling procedure twice more, marking the dough with four and then six indentations. (This simple trick will remind you where you are.) The dough is now ready to use. Bake this dough the same day, or it will lose its ability to rise in the oven. (Or form into the shape in which it is to be baked, and freeze for up to one month.) *Makes approximately 2½ pounds.*

· · · ◇ · · ·

PUFF DOUGH

Semidirect Method

· · ·

A D V A N C E D

2¼ pounds (7¼ cups) all-purpose flour
1 ounce (4 teaspoons) salt
1 pint 2 ounces (2¼ cups) water
9 ounces (2¼ sticks) lightly salted butter, melted and cooled
1 pound (4 sticks) lightly salted butter, cold, cut into cubes

Before embarking on the semidirect method of making puff dough, be sure that you have a large enough work space: 5 feet long by at least 3 feet wide is ideal.

Place flour, salt, water, and melted butter in bowl of electric mixer. Mix by hand and then, using a dough hook, mix until combined. It will be messy and crumbly looking. On a lightly floured surface, form into a ball and cut a cross into the top. Cover with plastic and refrigerate for 30 minutes.

Place the cubes of butter side by side between two sheets of wax paper or plastic and tap several times with a rolling pin to soften slightly. Roll out into a 12-inch square. On a floured surface, roll dough into a 16-inch square and place the butter in the center, at right angles, so that a triangle of dough extends on each side. Fold the flaps of dough over the butter and seal with your fingers. (It should look like the back of a square envelope.) Roll into a rectangle 15 by 45 inches, dusting lightly with flour so that it does not stick to the pin. Fold in three into a 15-inch square. Roll lightly to make level. Turn dough so that fold is on your left. Roll dough away from you into a 15-by-45-inch oblong. Fold into a square and roll lightly to make level and seal. You have now completed two "single turns." Make two indentations in the dough with your finger, one under the other, to signify two turns. Wrap in plastic and refrigerate for 1 hour. Repeat the rolling, folding, and chilling steps twice more, marking the dough with four and then six indentations. The dough is now ready to use. Makes approximately 5 pounds of dough; which will keep in the refrigerator for four days.

· · · ◇ · · ·

PUFF DOUGH

Direct or Classic Method

. . .

ADVANCED

2¼ pounds (7¼ cups) all-purpose flour
1 ounce (4 teaspoons) salt
1 pint 2 ounces (2¼ cups) water
1 pound 9 ounces (6¼ sticks) lightly salted butter, cut into cubes

Place flour, salt, and water in bowl of electric mixer. Mix by hand and then, using a dough hook, mix until combined but not yet smooth. Gather dough together and place on a lightly floured surface. Form into a ball and cut a cross in the top. Refrigerate for 30 minutes. (The dough must be chilled to the same temperature as the butter.)

Place cubes of butter side by side between two sheets of wax paper or plastic. Tap several times with a rolling pin to soften slightly. Roll out into a 10-inch square. On a lightly floured surface, roll dough into a 12-by-24-inch rectangle. Place the butter on the upper two-thirds. Fold flap of dough up and over butter; then fold top third down. Roll lightly to flatten and seal; then turn dough over. Roll out to approximately 30 by 12 inches, dusting lightly with flour as necessary to prevent sticking. Fold in three, like a business letter. Roll lightly to make level and seal. Give a quarter turn to the left so that the fold is perpendicular to you. Again roll the dough away from you into an even 30-by-12-inch rectangle, fold in three, and roll lightly to make level. You have now completed two "single turns." Make two indentations in the dough with your finger, one under the other, to signify two turns. Wrap in plastic and refrigerate for 1 hour or longer. Repeat the rolling, folding, and chilling twice more, making six turns in all. (All steps need not be completed in one day.) The dough is now ready to roll out and bake. Makes approximately 5 pounds of dough, which will keep in the refrigerator for four days.

· · · ◇ · · ·

PUFF DOUGH

Inversée (Butter Outside) Method

· · ·

ADVANCED

As with the direct and semidirect methods, this dough can be made in stages, over the course of a couple of days if necessary. For this reason, we make indentations in the chilled dough to indicate the number of "turns" it has received. This dough gets one double turn, two single turns, and a second double turn, making six turns in all, and must be well chilled between the stages.

2¼ pounds (7¼ cups) all-purpose flour
1 ounce (4 teaspoons) salt
¾ pint (1½ cups) water
1 pound 9 ounces (6¼ sticks) lightly salted butter, cold, cubed

Set aside 9 ounces (1¾ cups) of the flour to mix with the butter. Place remaining flour, salt, and water, in bowl of electric mixer. Mix by hand and then, using a dough hook, mix until combined. It will be messy and crumbly looking. Gather into a ball and let rest on a floured baking sheet while preparing butter.

Place butter and remaining flour in bowl of mixer and beat with flat beater until more or less incorporated. It will look rough. On a floured surface, roll into a 24-by-12-inch rectangle and let rest for 10 minutes.

Place flour-and-water rectangle on top of butter-and-flour rectangle, pulling a little if necessary to get both layers the same size. Push

··

against the sides of this double layer with a rolling pin to make even. Make a "double turn" by folding both sides toward the center, like a book. Fold again to "close the book." Flatten lightly with pin to make level and seal edges. Using two fingers, make a double indentation in dough to indicate that one double turn has been made. Wrap dough in plastic and refrigerate for 1 hour.

With the fold to your left, roll dough away from you into a 36-by-12-inch rectangle. Fold in three to form a square and roll lightly with pin to make even. Make a double indentation with a single indentation underneath to show that you have made one double and one single turn. Wrap in plastic and refrigerate for 1 hour. Repeat the single turn, mark dough with a double and two single indentations, and chill for 1 hour.

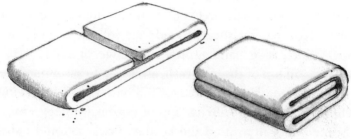

With the fold to your left, again roll dough away from you into a 36-by-12-inch rectangle. Fold both ends toward the middle and then fold dough in half, to make a double turn. Roll lightly with pin to make even. Make one double, two single, and one double indentation in the dough to signify the type and number of turns made, wrap in plastic, and refrigerate for 2 hours. The dough is now ready to roll out and bake. Makes approximately 4½ pounds of extra-fine dough, which will keep in the refrigerator for five days without losing its "puff" quality when baked.

· · · ◊ · · ·

PUFF DOUGH
TART SHELLS
. . .

2½ pounds puff dough of choice (recipes, pages 66 through 71)
1 egg yolk, for glaze
1 tablespoon cold water

Line a baking sheet with baking parchment. On a lightly floured surface, roll dough into a rectangle approximately 20 by 10 inches. Cut out two 9-inch-diameter circles and two strips ¾ inch wide by 14 inches long. Roll each circle out a little, to make it slightly larger, and place on a baking sheet. Blend egg yolk with cold water and brush a ¾-inch-wide band around the edge of each circle. Place dough strips on top of the egg wash, adjusting to accommodate circle and trimming length to fit exactly. Chill pastry shell for 20 minutes.

Preheat oven to 350°F. Brush top of border with egg wash. Make light slanted cuts all around the border. Prick bottom of shell and through border with a fork or cake tester. Bake for 20 minutes, until golden, and then fill with fruit of choice (see chapter on tarts) or fill first and then bake, accoording to recipe. *Makes two 9-inch tart shells.*

. . . ◊ . . .

VOL AU VENT

("Puffs of Wind" or Patty Shells)

. . .

2 pounds puff dough of choice (recipes, pages 66 through 71)
1 egg yolk, for glaze
1 tablespoon water

Line a baking sheet with baking parchment. On a lightly floured surface, roll dough ⅛ inch thick. With a fluted cutter, cut out twelve 3½-inch circles. Using a 2¼-inch cutter, remove the centers from half of the circles, making "doughnut" shapes. (Reserve trimmings and centers for another use, such as Allumettes, page 77.)

Place the solid circles on a baking sheet. Blend egg yolk with water. Brush over circles, being careful not to let it drip down the sides, as this would prevent the dough from rising properly. Place a "doughnut" on top of each circle of dough to form the sides of the patty shell. Chill shells for 20 minutes. Preheat oven to 350°F. Brush tops with egg wash. Prick the bottoms of the shells well. Bake for 20 to 25 minutes, until well puffed and golden. *Makes 6.*

VARIATION: The technique is slightly different for a Large Vol au Vent, as the shell is baked with a base, sides, and a very thin top. After baking, the top is carefully removed, the shell is filled and the top replaced, usually at a slight angle to show the ingredients within.

Roll out 2½ pounds of puff dough ⅛ thick. Cut out two 10-inch-diameter circles. Place an 8-inch-diameter cake pan on top of one of the circles, and cut around it to form a band of pastry for the sides of the Vol au Vent. Reserve the 8-inch-diameter circle for the top.

Place the larger solid circle of dough on the baking sheet. Brush a 1¾-inch-wide band of egg wash around the edge. Set the 2-inch-wide circular band of dough on top. Roll the reserved 8-inch-diameter circle of dough very thinly, to 10 inches in diameter. Carefully place on top of the Vol au Vent and secure the edges with light finger pressure. The center area will droop down a little, but will not stick to the bottom, as it is free of egg wash. Chill for 20 minutes.

Preheat oven to 350°F. Brush the entire top with egg wash, being careful not to let it drip down the sides. Make three little holes in the center, right through to the bottom of the dough. With a sharp knife, very lightly score a crisscross pattern over the center area. Bake for 25 minutes, or until well puffed and golden. *A filled Vol au Vent of this size will serve 8.*

· · · ◊ · · ·

APPLE CHAUSSONS
· · ·

INTERMEDIATE

These are puff dough turnovers with apple filling.

3 medium (1 pound total) Golden Delicious apples
1½ ounces (3 tablespoons) butter
1½ ounces (3 tablespoons) sugar
2½ pounds puff dough of choice (recipes, pages 66 through 71)
1 egg yolk, for glaze
1 tablespoon water

Peel and core apples and cut into dice. Melt the butter in a skillet and add the diced apple and the sugar. Sauté for 5 to 8 minutes until the apple cubes start to caramelize. Let cool.

Line a baking sheet with baking parchment. On a lightly floured surface, roll out dough ⅛ inch thick. Cut out six 5-inch-diameter rounds. Elongate each round into an oval by

pressing in center with a rolling pin, leaving both
ends "fatter." (See illustration.) Blend egg yolk
with water and brush edges of each pastry.
Place approximately 2 tablespoons of the
apple filling in the upper half of each.
Fold the dough over to form a half-circle
and seal the edges well with your fingers. Turn
pastries over and place on baking sheet. Chill for 20 minutes. Preheat
oven to 350°F. Brush tops with egg wash, being careful that it does
not run down the sides and prevent the dough from rising in the
oven. Prick a hole in each pastry for steam to escape, and score the
tops with a fern design. Bake for 25 minutes, until well puffed and
golden. *Makes 6.*

· · · ◊ · · ·

JAM TURNOVERS

· · ·

INTERMEDIATE

2½ pounds puff dough of choice (recipes, pages 66 through 71)
4 tablespoons raspberry, strawberry, or apricot jam
1 egg yolk for glaze
1 tablespoon water

Line a baking sheet with baking parchment. On a lightly floured
surface, roll out dough ⅛ inch thick and cut out six 6-inch squares.
Elongate the squares lightly into diamond shapes, running the rolling
pin slightly over the center but leaving the remaining triangle a little
"fatter." (See illustration.) Blend egg yolk with water and brush over
edges. Place 2 teaspoons of jam in center of each pastry. Fold the
"fatter" triangle of dough over the jam to form a triangular pastry

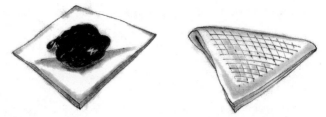

and press with fingers around edge to seal. Turn pastries over, transfer to a baking sheet, and chill for 20 minutes. Preheat oven to 350°F. Brush tops with egg wash and mark edges with a fork. Make a crosshatch pattern on the top of each by scoring lightly with a knife. Bake for 25 minutes, until well puffed and golden. *Makes 6.*

C H E E S E T W I S T S

. . .

E A S Y

1¼ pounds puff dough of choice (recipes, pages 66 through 71)
1 egg yolk, for glaze
1 tablespoon water
salt and pepper
6 ounces grated Swiss cheese

On a lightly floured surface, roll dough into a large rectangle approximately 18 by 16 inches. Trim edges and place on a baking sheet. Blend egg yolk with water and brush over dough. Season with salt and pepper and then sprinkle with grated cheese. Press lightly with a rolling pin to make the cheese stick. Cut dough into strips ¾ inch wide by 6 inches long, without separating. Let rest in refrigerator for 1½ hours.

To shape, fold each strip in half and then twist together into a rope, pinching the two ends to seal. Place on a baking sheet lined with baking parchment. Let rest in refrigerator for 30 minutes.

Preheat oven to 350°F. Bake cheese twists for 12 to 15 minutes, until golden and well puffed. *Makes approximately 60.*

· · · ◊ · · ·

A L L U M E T T E S

(Sugar Matchsticks)

· · ·

E A S Y

1¼ pounds puff dough of choice (recipes, pages 66 through 71)
6 ounces (1½ cups) confectioners' sugar
1 egg white, lightly beaten
dash vanilla extract
8 to 10 ounces (1 cup) sliced almonds
additional confectioners' sugar

On a lightly floured surface, roll out puff dough into two large rectangles, approximately 10 by 16 inches. Transfer to two lightly floured baking sheets and freeze for 30 minutes.

Preheat oven to 350°F. Line two baking sheets with baking parchment. Beat confectioners' sugar with just enough egg white to make a spreading consistency, and add a dash of vanilla. Spread the frozen dough with a thin layer of this icing. Cut dough into strips 4 by ¾ inches. (Slice dough with a chef's knife, wiping off blade after each cut to prevent icing from building up.) Scatter sliced almonds over top and sprinkle with confectioners' sugar. Separate the slices and transfer to prepared baking sheets. Bake for 20 minutes, or until crispy and lightly colored. *Makes approximately 80.*

··

PALMIERS

· · ·

Crisply caramelized Palmiers, or palm leaf cookies, should be quite brittle, and a shiny golden brown. You can make them any size you like, large or small, but the method of folding the dough is always the same.

18 ounces puff dough of choice (recipes, pages 66 through 71)
6 ounces (³/₄ cup), approximately sugar

Spread a thin layer of sugar on work surface. Roll dough on top of sugar into a 10-by-28-inch rectangle, turning dough over so that both sides have sugar on them. Trim edges straight and cut dough in half, making two 10-by-14-inch strips. Working with one strip at a time, fold both ends toward the middle, so that they almost meet at the center, like an open book. Sprinkle with sugar and fold again, "closing the book." Repeat with second strip. Freeze for 30 minutes.

Preheat oven to 350°F. Line two baking sheets with baking parchment. Cut dough into ¹/₂-inch-wide slices. Dip the flat sides of the cookies in sugar and place on baking sheets about 3 inches apart, cut side up. Bend the tips of the cookies outward. Bake for 20 minutes, until golden and starting to caramelize. Turn cookies over and bake for a further 5 minutes. *Makes approximately 40 Palmiers, 2³/₄ by 2¹/₂ inches.*

· · · ◇ · · ·

B A M B O O

. . .

To make these light, crisp pastries that look like bamboo, puff dough is stacked in layers and sliced. The slices expand sideways when baked, from 1/2 to 3 inches wide. When cool, they are sandwiched together with raspberry jam and decorated with bands of powdered sugar. This crunchy pastry is just outstanding with your morning coffee.

18 ounces puff dough of choice (recipes, pages 66 through 71)
1 egg yolk, for glaze
1 tablespoon water
raspberry jam
confectioners' sugar

Line two baking sheets with baking parchment. On a lightly floured surface, roll dough into a square about 21 by 21 inches and 1/8 inch thick. Trim edges of dough and cut into eight 10-by-5-inch rectangles. Blend egg yolk with water. Stack four slices on top of each other, brushing between layers with egg wash. Repeat with the other four slices. Roll the two stacks lightly to make the layers stick together. Freeze for 30 minutes.

Preheat oven to 350°F. Cut dough into slices 5 inches long and 1/2 inch thick. Lay the slices 4 inches apart on the prepared baking sheets, cut side facing up. Bake Bamboo for 25 minutes, or until puffed and golden. Let cool on racks. When cold, sandwich together in pairs with a thin layer of raspberry jam. Lay a 1-inch-wide strip of paper across the center of each pastry, at right angles to the direction of the "stripes," and dust with confectioners' sugar. Carefully remove paper. *Makes 10 double-layered pastries, 5 by 3 inches.*

. . . ◇ . . .

GÂTEAU NAPOLÉON

. . .

INTERMEDIATE

20 ounces puff dough of choice (recipes, pages 66 through 71)
3 cups Crème Mousseline (recipe, page 99)
1 tablespoon Cointreau
8 ounces (1 cup) generous sugar
⅓ cup water
4 ounces (½ cup) heavy cream
confectioners' sugar
sliced almonds, lightly toasted

Preheat oven to 350°F. Roll puff dough into an 11-by-16-inch rectangle, prick well so that it rises and bakes evenly, and bake for 25 minutes until golden. Let cool. Trim to 10 by 15 inches, and cut into three 10-by-5-inch rectangles.

Make Crème Mousseline, flavoring with Cointreau. Place one layer of pastry on a cake board and spread with 1 cup Crème. Top with second layer and spread with 1 cup Crème. Cover with third layer of pastry and spread sides with remaining Crème. Refrigerate while making caramel glaze.

In a heavy saucepan, preferably of unlined copper or stainless steel, heat sugar with water until it caramelizes, at 350°F. Stir in cream and let simmer for 2 minutes. Rub a long knife blade lightly with vegetable oil and hold the knife diagonally across cake from one corner to another to form a barrier. Pour caramel glaze over one half of the cake. Dust the other half generously with confectioners' sugar. Mask sides with sliced almonds, pressing lightly with a baker's spatula. (It is easiest to hold the cake over the tray of almonds, scattering the nuts with the other hand.) Refrigerate cake until ready to serve, which should be within 4 hours so that the pastry remains crisp. Cut with a serrated blade, using a light sawing motion. *Serves 8.*

G Â T E A U   P I T H I V I E R S

. . .

INTERMEDIATE

This crispy tart of glazed puff pastry has a filling of Almond Pastry Cream. It gets its name from the French town of Pithiviers.

2 pounds puff dough of choice (recipes, pages 66 through 71)
14 ounces (1¾ cups) Almond Pastry Cream filling (recipe, page 110)
2 tablespoons dark rum
1 egg yolk, for glaze
1 tablespoon cold water
confectioners' sugar

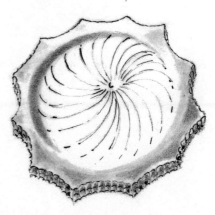

Line a baking sheet with baking parchment. On a lightly floured surface, roll puff dough out into a 24-by-12-inch rectangle. Using a cake pan as a guide, cut out two 10-inch circles. Place circles on the prepared baking sheet and refrigerate while making filling.

Make Almond Pastry Cream according to the recipe and beat in the rum. Blend egg yolk with water. Brush around edge of one of the circles of puff dough in a 2-inch-wide band. Place filling in center and spread to within 1 inch of edge, making an even layer about ½ inch thick. Top with the second circle of puff dough and press the edges down very well with your fingers. It is important that the pastry is well sealed, otherwise the filling will leak out during baking. Trim edges with a large round fluted cutter, making a series of half-moon-shaped cuts (see illustration). Chill tart for 20 minutes.

Preheat oven to 350°F. Brush top of tart with remaining egg wash, making sure that it does not drip down the sides and prevent the pastry from rising. Prick a tiny hole in the center for steam to escape.

. . . .

From the center, lightly cut spiral lines to the edge of the filling (see illustration).

Bake for 45 minutes, or until well risen and golden. Quickly sprinkle with confectioners' sugar and bake for a further 5 to 10 minutes, until well browned and glazed. *Serves 8.*

. . . ◊ . . .

4

Yeast-Raised Doughs

. . . ◇ . . .

Technically a by-product of beer-making, baker's yeast is a tiny plant that, given the right conditions, will multiply and create carbon dioxide gas as well as alcohol. When yeast is mixed with flour and water and left in a warm place, it combines with the gluten in the flour to create a weblike structure with many air spaces, or what we call a leavened dough.

I recommend using fresh baker's compressed yeast, not the dried granular kind, for the very best results. It is available in $^3/_5$-ounce cakes at most United States supermarkets, and must be kept refrigerated. One cake of this yeast is the equivalent of a $^1/_4$-ounce package of the dried granular variety. Never bring yeast into direct contact with sugar or salt. Sugar will cause overfermentation and create an off, "yeasty" flavor, while salt could kill it. Instead, protect the yeast by always adding flour at the same time.

In professional bakeries a proofing box is used when raising bread doughs. This is a form of airtight cupboard with adjustable heat and humidity controls. A temperature of between 80° and 92°F. is ideal. In the home kitchen, I suggest that you warm your oven to 100°F. and then turn the heat off. Put your dough on a floured baking sheet or in a warmed, greased bowl and place in the oven with a bowl of boiling water alongside. This will create a suitably warm, moist environment for the yeast. If it is not convenient to use your oven as a proofing box, simply place your dough and the bowl of boiling water on a countertop and cover both with a cardboard box. Replace the boiling water once or twice during the rising period. This is a somewhat rustic solution, but it works!

Fine yeast doughs such as Brioche and Panettone require a great deal *of kneading and it is not practical to attempt to make them without an electric mixer equipped with a dough hook. We have found that these breads have a better texture if made in relatively large quantities, as the dough hook cannot operate efficiently with too little dough. Incidentally, the dough hook on most domestic stand mixers was designed to knead doughs but not to mix the ingredients together in the first place. Instead, mix by hand to incorporate. Then knead with the dough hook.*

Index:

· · · ◇ · · ·

Yeast-Raised Doughs

CROISSANTS

. . .

18 ounces (3¾ cups) all-purpose flour
¾ ounce baker's compressed yeast
½ ounce (1 tablespoon) salt
2 ounces (¼ cup) generous sugar
8 ounces (1 cup) water
12 ounces (3 sticks) unsalted butter, at room temperature
1 egg yolk, for glaze
1 tablespoon water

In bowl of electric mixer, combine flour, yeast, salt, sugar, and water. Mix by hand and then beat with dough hook at medium speed for 10 minutes. Dough should be very smooth, and leave the sides of the bowl clean. Transfer dough to a lightly floured baking sheet and cover with greased plastic wrap. Let rise for 1½ hours at warm room temperature, about 70°F. Cut butter into cubes.

Place cubes of butter side by side between two sheets of plastic or wax paper. Tap several times with a rolling pin to soften slightly and roll out into a 12-inch square. On a lightly floured surface, roll dough into a 16-inch square and place the butter in the center at an angle, so that a triangle of dough extends on each side. Fold the flaps of dough over the butter and seal with your fingers. (It should look like the back of a square envelope.) Roll out very thinly to 24 by 18 inches and fold in three like a business letter. Give a quarter turn to the left and turn dough over. Again roll into a 24-by-18-inch rectangle, fold in three, and give a quarter turn to the left. Repeat once more, making three "single turns" in all. Refrigerate dough for 2 hours.

On a lightly floured surface, roll dough into a 11-by-16-inch rectangle. Fold to make a 5½-by-16-inch strip. Trim all four edges with a knife. Make slanting cuts to form 5-inch triangles and separate the two layers. You should now have 10 triangles. Roll each one toward the apex and bend the ends slightly to form a crescent or curve. Tuck the tail end underneath. Let rise at warm room temperature for 1 hour. Blend egg yolk with 1 tablespoon water and brush over croissants.

Preheat oven to 400°F. Bake croissants for 15 minutes, until well puffed and golden. *Makes 10.*

· · · ◇ · · ·

B R I O C H E   À   T Ê T E

· · ·

I N T E R M E D I A T E

For the very best results, make brioche dough and allow it to rest in the refrigerator overnight before forming and baking. It must be kneaded for a long time to develop the right texture, so be sure to start with cold eggs and cold water, or the dough will get too warm and melt the butter.

6 eggs, large, cold
4 ounces (½ cup) cold water
2 teaspoons orange flower water (page 3) or orange extract
1 pound 6 ounces (4½ cups) all-purpose flour
4 ounces (½ cup) sugar
1 ounce baker's compressed yeast
½ ounce (2 teaspoons) salt
8 ounces (2 sticks) unsalted butter, soft
1 egg yolk, for glaze
1 tablespoon cold water

In bowl of electric mixer, combine eggs, water, and orange flower water. Stir in flour, sugar, crumbled yeast, and salt. Mix by hand, then beat with a dough hook at medium speed until dough is very smooth and silky and clears side of bowl, about 25 minutes. Cut butter into bits and add a little at a time. Beat at medium speed for 10 minutes. You should *hear* your brioche—it will slap the sides of the bowl. Dough should become very silky and resilient. Place dough on a lightly floured baking sheet, cover with plastic, and let rise at 70°F.

until doubled in bulk, about 1 hour. Turn out onto a lightly floured surface and pat flat. Form into a ball and place in a large bowl. Cover and let rise in refrigerator overnight.

Turn dough out onto a lightly floured surface and roll flat. Roll dough into a cylinder and cut into 24 equal pieces, about 2 ounces each. With lightly floured hands, roll each into a ball and let rest for 10 minutes. Grease twenty-four 4-ounce fluted brioche molds with butter. Elongate each ball of dough slightly into a pear shape, making a "neck" with the heel of your hand. The "head" should form about one-third of the total size. Transfer dough to a mold, pressing around the "head" with your fingers so that it sits down within the main ball of dough. Repeat with remaining balls of dough and let rise in a warm place until dough reaches tops of molds, about 1 hour.

Preheat oven to 375°F. Blend egg yolk with 1 tablespoon cold water and brush over tops of brioches. Try not to get the glaze on the molds, as it may make the brioches stick. Place molds on a baking sheet and bake for 15 minutes, until well risen and glossy brown. Serve warm. *Makes 24.*

N O T E : Brioche can be frozen. Allow to thaw, then heat before serving. Leftover brioche is delicious sliced and lightly toasted, or it can be used in desserts such as the Diplomat (recipe, page 103).

· · · ◊ · · ·

S A V A R I N
A N D   R U M   B A B A S
· · ·

I N T E R M E D I A T E

A large savarin and individual babas are made from the same dough. Traditionally, the savarin is saturated with a Kirsch-flavored Simple Syrup, brushed with Apricot Glaze, and decorated with candied fruits. The center of the ring is usually filled with Crème Chantilly. Babas are generally soaked with rum-flavored syrup and then brushed with Apricot Glaze. Naturally, you may choose whichever flavoring you prefer; Cognac is good too. Both the savarin and the small babas can be baked and then frozen. Defrost thoroughly before saturating with warm syrup. This recipe makes enough dough to fill one 8½-inch-diameter savarin mold and four 2-inch-high, 3-ounce baba or timbale molds, or sixteen baba molds.

Cake:

10 ounces (2 cups) all-purpose flour
2 ounces (¼ cup) generous sugar
pinch salt
½ ounce baker's compressed yeast
2 ounces (¼ cup) milk
2 ounces (¼ cup) water
2 eggs, large
4 ounces (1 stick) unsalted butter, melted

Syrup:

1 pint (2 cups) Simple Syrup (recipe, page 237)
6 ounces (¾ cup) Kirsch or rum

Glaze:

4 ounces (½ cup) Apricot Glaze (recipe, page 241)

Decoration:

glacé cherries, angelica, orange peel (optional)
2 cups Crème Chantilly (recipe, page 99)

In bowl of electric mixer, combine flour, sugar, salt, crumbled yeast, milk, water, and eggs. Combine by hand, then beat with flat beater at low-medium speed until dough is smooth, shiny, and elastic, about 10 minutes. Add lukewarm butter and beat for 5 minutes. The dough will be almost liquid. Let rise in a warm place (see page 83 for my recommendations on proofing yeast doughs in a domestic kitchen) until doubled in bulk, about 1 hour.

Butter an 8½-inch-diameter savarin mold and four 3-ounce baba molds. Pull out "strings" of dough and place balls of dough side by side in mold. It should be filled about one-half full. Divide remaining dough among the buttered baba molds. Let rise in a warm place until dough reaches the top of molds, about 30 minutes.

Preheat oven to 375°F. Bake savarin for about 30 minutes, until well browned and risen. Remove babas after 15 minutes. Unmold onto a rack.

Place the savarin in a shallow dish slightly larger than the cake. Spoon the Kirsch syrup, which should be lukewarm, over the savarin little by little, so that as much syrup as possible is absorbed, but the cake retains its shape. Let drain on rack for 15 minutes. Brush savarin with Apricot Glaze and arrange a few candied fruits on top, if you wish. Place cake on a suitable serving dish and fill the center with Crème Chantilly. *Serves 8.*

RUM BABAS: Proceed as for savarin, but substitute dark rum for Kirsch in the syrup. Babas can be served plain or with Crème Chantilly, and of course they too may be decorated with candied fruit if you wish.

· · · ◊ · · ·

K U G E L H O P F

. . .

An Austrian specialty, this yeast-raised cake seems to have become richer and heavier at other bakeries over the years. My version is more like the original: a lightly sweetened bread dough with raisins and orange peel added.

8 ounces (1 cup) milk
1 pound (3¼ cups) all-purpose flour
4 ounces (½ cup) sugar
¼ teaspoon salt
¾ ounces baker's compressed yeast
2 eggs, large, at room temperature
4 ounces (1 stick) unsalted butter, melted
1 tablespoon butter, soft but not melted, for mold
2 tablespoons sliced almonds for mold
1 orange
8 ounces (1⅓ cups) raisins (dark or yellow, or half of each)
confectioners' sugar

Heat milk to lukewarm. In bowl of electric mixer, combine flour, sugar, salt, and crumbled yeast. Beat the eggs lightly with the warm milk and stir into flour mixture by hand. Place bowl on mixer stand and beat with the dough hook at medium speed for 5 minutes. Add melted, lukewarm butter a little at a time and beat at low speed until incorporated. Then beat at medium speed for 10 minutes. Turn dough into a warmed, dry bowl, cover with plastic, and let rise until doubled in bulk, 45 minutes to 1 hour. (See page 83 for best rising techniques to use in a home kitchen.)

Brush the bottom, sides, and central tube of a 2-quart fluted Kugelhopf mold evenly with soft butter. Do this with care, so that the Kugelhopf will unmold perfectly. Sprinkle bottom and sides of mold with almonds. Pare the colored part only from the orange and chop very finely. Mix minced orange peel with the raisins.

Turn dough out onto a lightly floured surface. Pat flat and knead in the raisins and orange peel. Form dough into a ball and make a hole in the center with two fingers, forming a large doughnut shape. Place ring of dough in prepared mold and let rise until it reaches to within 1 inch of top of mold. This will take approximately 30 minutes in a warm environment.

Preheat oven to 375°F. (Remember to remove dough if you are using your oven as a proofing box. It will continue rising in the warm mold.) Bake Kugelhopf for about 40 minutes, until well browned and firm. If top browns too quickly, cover loosely with a sheet of aluminum foil. Let stand for 2 minutes, then unmold and cool on rack. Dust with confectioners' sugar before serving. *Serves 8.*

NOTE: Kugelhopf will keep for several days if stored airtight, and can be frozen successfully. Slightly stale Kugelhopf is delicious when sliced and soaked in warm Simple Syrup (recipe, page 237) flavored with rum.

5.

Custards & Creams;
Custard Desserts

· · · ◇ · · ·

Confectioners' Custard is a simple mixture of eggs, sugar, flour, and milk, flavored with vanilla. I recommend using a whole vanilla bean rather than vanilla extract, as the flavor is more mellow. After infusing in milk, remove the bean and rinse it in water. Dry and store in a container full of sugar. This will both flavor the sugar and preserve the bean, which can be reused until the flavor fades.

Confectioners' Custard can be used just as it is to fill cakes, tarts, and pastries, or can be made richer—or lighter—with the further addition of egg yolks, egg whites, whipped cream, or unsalted butter. It is usually flavored with some kind of liqueur, chocolate, coffee, or Praliné Paste. These rich and creamy fillings are pretty much interchangeable, according to your taste.

Crème Anglaise is the classic light "pouring consistency" custard used as a dessert sauce, and is made without flour. Crème Caramel is a smooth custard dessert that is baked in the oven. A Bavarois is a molded Crème Anglaise made with the addition of gelatin and cream.

Generally speaking, it is important to have all pastry cream ingredients at the same temperature and consistency so that they blend properly. Always stir in your flavorings before adding butter or cream. Use only the best-quality liqueurs: a little goes a long way. (Cheap brands will break down your creams and tend to leave a "hot" aftertaste.)

Index:

· · · ◇ · · ·

Custards & Creams;
Custard Desserts

CONFECTIONERS'
CUSTARD

. . .

E A S Y

Confectioners' Custard is used as a smooth and creamy filling for tarts, éclairs, napoléons, and so on, and as a base for more elaborate pastry creams. It will keep in the refrigerator for three days.

When making large amounts of Confectioners' Custard in my bakery, I mix the sugar with the flour and beat in the eggs using a large and powerful commercial mixer. Then the mixture is combined with boiling milk in the usual way. I give you here a slightly different method, for use in the home kitchen, as it gives better results when working with small amounts of custard.

2 ounces (¼ cup) generous sugar
2 egg yolks, large
1 ounce (¼ cup) all-purpose flour, sifted
10 ounces (1¼ cups) milk
3-inch piece vanilla bean

Place sugar and egg yolks in a mixing bowl and beat until pale and thick. Beat in sifted flour. Put milk in saucepan with vanilla bean and heat to boiling. Remove and save bean. Pour half of the boiling milk into the egg yolk mixture. Stir quickly and pour combined mixture back into saucepan. Whisk vigorously over low-medium heat until custard boils, thickens, and turns shiny. (Be sure to cook long enough to thoroughly cook the flour.) Pour custard into a bowl. To prevent a skin from forming as custard cools, dust with confectioners' sugar or "paint" lightly with a cube of butter. *Makes approximately 1½ cups.*

. . . ◇ . . .

VARIOUS FLAVORINGS FOR CONFECTIONERS' CUSTARD

Pastry creams can be flavored according to taste, and purpose. For each pint of custard, choose one of the following:

½ ounce (1 tablespoon) Kirsch
                        Cognac
                        Grand Marnier
                        Cointreau
                        Kahlúa
                        dark rum
                        English gin
                        Scotch whisky
2 tablespoons Praliné Paste (recipe, page 248)
2 ounces (2 squares) unsweetened chocolate, melted
½ ounce (¼ cup) instant coffee powder, dissolved
    in a little hot water

· · · ◊ · · ·

CRÈME LIEGEOISE
(Confectioners' Custard with Whipped Cream)

· · ·

EASY

¾ pint (1½ cups) Confectioners' Custard
    (recipe, page 95)
flavoring of choice
4 ounces (½ cup) heavy cream, whipped

Have Confectioners' Custard at room temperature. Stir in flavoring and fold in cream. *Makes approximately 3½ cups.*

CRÈME LÉGÈRE

*(Light Confectioners' Custard with
Egg Whites and Gelatin)*

. . .

EASY

¼ ounce (1 envelope) unflavored gelatin
1 tablespoon cold water
8 ounces (1 cup) Confectioners' Custard (recipe, page 95)
1 egg yolk, large
1 tablespoon flavoring of choice
3 egg whites, large
1 ounce (2 tablespoons) sugar

Dissolve gelatin in cold water and let stand for 5 minutes. Place custard in a saucepan, stir in egg yolk, and bring to a boil. Immediately add gelatin and let simmer for a few seconds, stirring. Remove from heat and stir in flavoring. Beat egg whites until soft peaks form. Slowly add sugar and then beat at high speed until stiff and shiny. Fold into warm custard. *Makes approximately 3½ cups.*

. . . ◇ . . .

CRÈME CHIBOUSTE

(Light Confectioners' Custard with Gelatin and Butter)

. . .

EASY

¼ ounce (1 envelope) unflavored gelatin
1 tablespoon cold water
8 ounces (1 cup) Confectioners' Custard (recipe, page 95)
1 egg yolk, large
1 tablespoon dark rum
2 ounces (½ stick) unsalted butter, soft and creamy
3 egg whites, large
2 ounces (¼ cup) generous sugar

Dissolve gelatin in cold water and let stand for 5 minutes. Place custard in a saucepan, stir in egg yolk, and bring to a boil. Immediately add gelatin and let simmer for a few seconds, stirring. Remove from heat. Whisk in rum and creamy butter. Beat egg whites until soft peaks start to form. Add sugar slowly and then beat at high speed with sugar until stiff and glossy. Fold into warm custard. *Makes approximately 3½ cups.*

. . . ◇ . . .

CRÈME MOUSSELINE

(Rich Confectioners' Custard with Butter)

. . .

EASY

1 pint (2 cups) Confectioners' Custard (recipe, page 95)
1 tablespoon flavoring of choice
8 ounces (2 sticks) unsalted butter, soft and creamy

Have Confectioners' Custard at room temperature. Add flavoring and beat in butter, little by little. *Makes approximately 3 cups.*

. . . ◊ . . .

CRÈME CHANTILLY

(Whipped Cream with Sugar and Vanilla)

. . .

EASY

1 pint (2 cups) heavy cream
1 teaspoon vanilla extract
4 ounces (1 cup) confectioners' sugar, sifted

Beat cream until it starts to thicken. Beat in vanilla and confectioners' sugar. *Makes approximately 3⅓ cups.*

. . . ◊ . . .

CRÈME ANGLAISE

(Light Custard Sauce)

. . .

EASY

1 pint (2 cups) milk
1 vanilla bean
4 egg yolks, large
4 ounces (½ cup) sugar

Place milk in a saucepan with vanilla bean and heat to boiling. Remove and save bean. Beat yolks with sugar until a pale, thick emulsion is formed. Pour half the boiling milk into the egg yolk mixture. Stir quickly and pour the combined mixture back into the saucepan. Stir with a wooden spatula until the mixture thickens slightly and reaches 165°F. It should coat the back of the spatula. Pour through a sieve into a bowl and let cool. Crème Anglaise will keep for two or three days in the refrigerator. *Makes approximately 3 cups.*

. . . ◊ . . .

CUSTARD CARAMEL SAUCE

(Crème Anglaise with Caramel Flavoring)

. . .

EASY

8 ounces (1 cup) generous sugar
4 ounces (½ cup) water
8 ounces (1 cup) Crème Anglaise, warm

Boil sugar and water together, preferably in an unlined copper pot, until mixture starts to turn a deep golden-tan color and reaches 350°F. on a candy thermometer. Remove from heat and stir into warm Crème Anglaise. Transfer to sauceboat and serve warm. *Makes 1½ cups.*

CRÈME BAVAROIS
(Crème Anglaise with Gelatin and Cream)

. . .

EASY

This custard can be unmolded or not, as you prefer. Various flavorings may be added, such as those listed on page 96, before adding the whipped cream.

½ ounce (2 envelopes) unflavored gelatin
1 pint (2 cups) milk
1 vanilla bean
4 egg yolks, large
4½ ounces (½ cup) generous sugar
10 ounces (1¼ cups) heavy cream

Soften gelatin in cold water. Place milk in a saucepan with vanilla bean and heat to boiling. Remove and save bean. Beat yolks with sugar until a smooth, light-colored emulsion is formed. Pour half the boiling milk into the egg yolks. Stir quickly and pour combined mixture back into the pan. Stir with a wooden spatula until the mixture thickens slightly and reaches 165°F. Add gelatin and stir over heat for a few seconds. Pour through a sieve into a bowl and let cool. When cold, stir in flavoring of choice and fold in whipped cream. Pour into a 1½-quart mold and refrigerate until set, about 4 hours. *Makes 5 cups*

. . . ◊ . . .

· ·

CRÈME CARAMEL
RENVERSÉE

(Baked Custard with Caramel Topping)

. . .

EASY

These individual custards are baked in a bain marie (use a shallow roasting pan half-filled with water), then chilled and unmolded. The caramelized sugar in the bottom of the custard cups, which is softened by the custard, will form a sauce.

Caramel:

8 ounces (1 cup) generous sugar
4 ounces (½ cup) water

Custard:

5 eggs, large
4½ ounces (½ cup) generous sugar
1 pint (2 cups) milk
1 vanilla bean

Preheat oven to 350°F. Butter four 8-ounce custard cups.

TO MAKE CARAMEL: Boil sugar and water together over medium-high heat until the mixture starts to turn a deep golden-tan color, 350°F. on a candy thermometer. Quickly pour a little into the bottom of each custard cup, swirling to spread around. The caramel will harden almost at once.

TO MAKE CUSTARD: Beat eggs with sugar until light and lemon-colored. Put milk in a saucepan with the vanilla bean and heat to boiling. Remove and save bean. Pour milk over the egg-sugar mixture and mix well.

Place custard cups in roasting pan and fill each with custard, pouring it through a fine sieve. Put pan on oven rack and fill with enough boiling water to reach halfway up sides of cups. Cover loosely with aluminum foil and bake for 40 minutes, or until set. A knife blade inserted in the custard should come out clean. Remove from pan and chill thoroughly. Unmold before serving. *Serves 4. (Recipe can be doubled.)*

. . . ◊ . . .

D I P L O M A T   I N   P A S T R Y

(Pastry Shell, Sponge Cake, Candied Peel, and Custard)

. . .

E A S Y

This is a very good way to use up sponge cake trimmings, left over after making other cakes, or day-old brioche. You will need about 4 cups of broken-up cake to lightly fill the pastry shell.

1¼ pounds Pâte Sucrée or Pâte Brisée (recipes, pages 25 through 27)
12 ounces (4 cups) sponge cake trimmings
6 ounces (1 cup) chopped mixed candied peel or raisins, or a mixture of both
7 eggs, large
6 ounces (¾ cups) scant sugar
1½ pints (3 cups) milk
1 teaspoon vanilla extract
4 ounces (½ cup) Apricot Glaze (recipe, page 241) (optional)

Preheat oven to 375°F. Butter a 9-inch cake pan. On a lightly floured surface, roll out sugar dough of choice ⅛ inch thick. Line cake pan, fitting pastry against bottom and sides without stretching the dough. Cut off excess at rim level.

Fill pastry shell lightly with layers of broken-up cake, scattering each layer with chopped candied fruit and raisins. Place eggs and sugar in a bowl and whisk until well blended. Whisk in milk and vanilla. Slowly pour this custard mixture over the cake, letting it soak in well. Bake for 60 minutes, or until custard is firm and pastry is well browned. Let cool in pan and turn out. Brush with Apricot Glaze if desired. Serve at room temperature. *Serves 8.*

6.

Buttercreams

· · · ◇ · · ·

Classic buttercreams can be made with egg yolks, egg whites, whole eggs, or Crème Anglaise combined with sugar and unsalted butter. Variously flavored with liqueurs, Praliné Paste, chocolate, or coffee, they are used to fill cakes and pastries. While it is true that ersatz imitations made with whipped vegetable fats and egg whites are widely used by many commercial bakeries, for reasons of economy, they have a very unpleasant texture and flavor and are to be avoided.

Buttercream made with egg yolks will keep for two or three days in the refrigerator. Made with egg whites, it will keep for six days; with Crème Anglaise or Sabayon, three days.

· · · ◇ · · ·

Index:

· · · ◇ · · ·

Buttercreams

BUTTERCREAM I,

with Egg Yolks

· · ·

The trick to achieving a good liaison with the egg yolks and sugar syrup is first, not to get the sugar syrup too hot, or it will harden when it hits the egg yolks, and second, to add it in a very slow, thin stream. Even the best of the domestic-sized electric stand mixers spatter too much when you do this, so it is best to add the syrup to the yolks while beating them by hand, either with a whisk or a hand-held electric mixer. Then transfer the mixture to the stand mixer for beating until well aerated and cooled, which takes a good 10 to 15 minutes.

8 ounces (1 cup) sugar
2½ ounces (5 tablespoons) water
5 egg yolks, large
1 tablespoon flavoring of choice (see list of flavorings
    for Confectioners' Custard, page 96)
9 ounces (2¼ sticks) unsalted butter, soft

Combine sugar and water in a heavy saucepan of unlined copper or stainless steel. Boil to 250°F., or hard ball stage. Place egg yolks in bowl of electric mixer and beat until light with whisk or hand-held electric mixer. While beating vigorously, pour in sugar syrup in a *thin* stream, being careful not to pour it down the sides of the bowl or onto the beater. Set mixer bowl on stand and beat with wire whip at medium speed until a complete emulsion is formed, and the mixture is cold. Beat in flavoring of choice. At low speed, beat in butter little by little. When completely incorporated, beat at high speed for a few seconds. *Makes approximately 3 cups.*

· · · ◊ · · ·

BUTTERCREAM II,
with Egg Whites

· · ·

INTERMEDIATE

3 egg whites, large
6 ounces (¾ cup) scant sugar
2 ounces (¼ cup) water
1 tablespoon flavoring of choice (see list of flavorings
  for Confectioners' Custard, page 96)
9 ounces (2¼ sticks) unsalted butter, soft

Place egg whites in a mixer bowl and beat until stiff. Cook sugar and water to the hard ball stage, 250°F., and proceed exactly as for Buttercream I. *Makes approximately 2 cups.*

· · · ◊ · · ·

BUTTERCREAM III,
with Crème Anglaise

· · ·

INTERMEDIATE

4 ounces (½ cup) milk
3-inch piece vanilla bean
7 ounces (¾ cup) generous sugar
6 egg yolks, large
1 tablespoon flavoring of choice (see list of flavorings
  for Confectioners' Custard, page 96)
10 ounces (2½ sticks) unsalted butter, soft

Place milk and vanilla bean in a saucepan and heat to boiling. Remove bean. Beat egg yolks with sugar until a smooth, light emulsion is formed. Pour half the boiling milk into the egg-sugar mixture, whisking vigorously. Pour combined mixture back into saucepan. Whisk over medium heat until custard thickens and reaches 165°F. (It should coat the back of a wooden spoon.) Pour through a sieve into a bowl and let cool. To prevent a skin from forming, "paint" the surface with a cube of butter. When cold, add flavoring and beat in butter, little by little. *Makes approximately 3½ cups.*

· · · ◇ · · ·

BUTTERCREAM IV,

with Sabayon

· ·

INTERMEDIATE

Sabayon is a light wine custard, widely known in Italian cuisine as Za-baglione, made by beating eggs and sugar over heat until they expand and form a liaison.

3 eggs, large
6 ounces (¾ cup) scant sugar
1 tablespoon flavoring of choice (see list of flavorings
   for Confectioners' Custard, page 96)
9 ounces (2¼ sticks) unsalted butter, soft

Combine eggs and sugar in a bowl, preferably of unlined copper. Beat over simmering water until light and fluffy, and mixture is warm to the touch. Remove from heat and beat until cold. Add flavoring and beat in butter, little by little. *Makes approximately 2 cups.*

ALMOND PASTRY CREAM

(Pâte d'Amandes)

. . .

Almond Pastry Cream is used as a tart filling, and is always baked. It will keep in the refrigerator in its uncooked state for two days.

8 ounces (1 cup) generous sugar

9 ounces (2¼ cups) almond meal (page 1)

8 ounces (2 sticks) unsalted butter, soft

4 eggs, large

1 ounce (¼ cup) all-purpose flour

In bowl of electric mixer, combine sugar and almond meal. Add butter and beat with flat beater until very light and creamy. Add eggs one by one, beating well after each addition. Stir in flour last. *Makes approximately 2 cups.*

N O T E : Almond Pastry Cream can be made in a food processor, but it will not be as light.

7.
Afternoon Tea &
Plain Cakes
(Without Fillings)

· · · ◊ · · ·

These relatively plain cakes are perfect when served with afternoon tea. Some, such as my Apple Cake, are also very good for breakfast, or with morning coffee; others, like the Walnut Cake with Coffee Sauce, are suitable for dessert. It all depends on personal taste and inclination.

The presentation of this kind of cake is always simple: at most they get a dusting of confectioners' sugar and perhaps a nutmeat or two to indicate the flavor within.

Index:

· · · ◊ · · ·

Afternoon Tea &
Plain Cakes
(Without Fillings)

Apple Cake
Orange Loaf Cake
Buttermilk Chocolate Cake
Savannah Loaf Cake
Walnut Cake with Coffee Sauce
Flourless Chocolate-Walnut Cake
Flourless Almond Cake with Frozen Eggs
Flourless Chocolate-Almond Cake with Frozen Eggs

APPLE CAKE

. . .

I like to eat this light cake at breakfast time with café *au lait . . . and so do the customers in my bakeries. I always bake it in oval pans, but these are hard to find, and of course a round one will do instead. To get even apple slices for the top, cut the peeled apple in half and take out the core with a melon baller. Then cut across in* 1/4-*inch thick slices.*

3 medium (1 pound) Golden Delicious apples
8 ounces (2 sticks) unsalted butter, soft
8 ounces (1 cup) generous sugar
3 eggs, large
1 egg yolk, large
4 ounces (¾ cup) scant all-purpose flour
½ teaspoon baking powder
3 ounces (6 tablespoons) milk, lukewarm
½ teaspoon vanilla extract

Preheat oven to 360°F. Butter and flour an 8-inch round or oval cake pan.

Peel and core the apples. Dice two of them and cut the third into 1/4-inch-thick slices. Melt 2 tablespoons of the butter in a skillet and add the diced apples. Sprinkle with 2 tablespoons of the sugar and let cook, stirring often, for 7 to 8 minutes, until liquid has evaporated and apples are starting to caramelize. Let cool to lukewarm.

In bowl of electric mixer, combine remaining butter and sugar. Beat with paddle for 10 minutes, until mixture is white and very creamy. Add eggs and egg yolk one at a time, beating well after each addition. Sift flour and baking powder together and pour around edge of bowl. Beat until a smooth emulsion is formed. Add milk and vanilla extract and mix until smooth. Spread half the batter in the prepared cake pan and cover with drained, diced apple (do not add butter from the pan). Cover with rest of batter. Place raw sliced apple in an overlapping circle on top of cake, like a wreath. Bake for 45 minutes, or until cake is golden and a skewer inserted in the center comes out clean. Unmold and cool on rack. *Serves 8.*

· · · ◇ · · ·

ORANGE LOAF CAKE
· · ·

EASY

This cake is somewhat like a pound cake, but much lighter and finer in texture. It's important to add your orange zest at the last minute or the citrus oil might flatten your batter.

1 orange, peel only
3 eggs, large
6 ounces (¾ cup) scant sugar
dash salt
6 ounces (1¼ cups) scant all-purpose flour
1 teaspoon baking powder
2 ounces (½ stick) unsalted butter, soft and creamy
2½ ounces (5 tablespoons) heavy cream
1 tablespoon dark rum
confectioners' sugar

Preheat oven to 350°F. Butter and flour an 8-by-4½-inch loaf pan.
Pare colored part of peel from orange and chop very finely. Set aside. In bowl of electric mixer, combine eggs, sugar, and salt. Beat with whisk until pale and fluffy. Add flour and baking powder and mix well. Add butter and beat until a complete emulsion is formed; the batter must be very light and creamy. Beat in cream and rum, and finally add orange zest. Spoon batter into prepared loaf pan, smoothing the top. Bake for 45 minutes, until a skewer inserted in the center comes out clean. Unmold and cool on a rack. Dust with confectioners' sugar before serving. *Serves 8.*

Clockwise from top:
TRADITIONAL FRENCH STYLE
APPLE TART,
STRAWBERRY AND
RASPBERRY TARTS
PREPARED ON
TARTE EXOTIQUE BASE

P I N E A P P L E   C R O W N   C A K E

A N D

V A L E N C I A   C A K E

Clockwise from top:

STRAWBERRY PINSTRIPE CAKE,

JESTER CAKE,

ARLEQUIN CAKE

Clockwise from top:

PALMIERS, MACAROONS,

RASPBERRY WINDOW COOKIES,

ALLUMETTES, DUCHESSE COOKIES,

CIGARETTES, BÂTONS DE MARÉCHAL

Clockwise from upper right:

ORANGE LOAF CAKE,

APPLE CAKE,

FLOURLESS CHOCOLATE-ALMOND CAKE

WITH FROZEN EGGS

Clockwise from top:

ROUND GÂTEAU MARRON,

BÛCHE DE NOËL,

PANETTONE

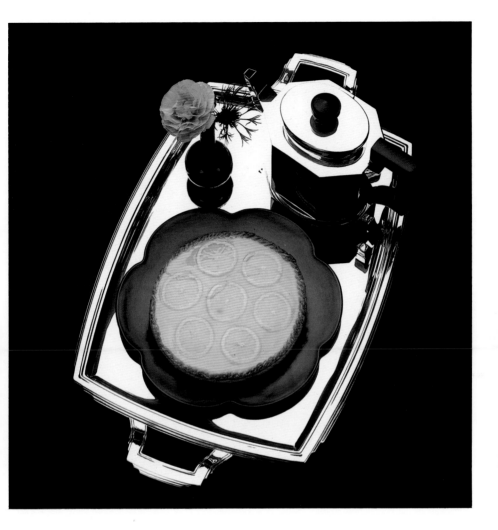

LEMON CUSTARD TART

From top to bottom:
BAMBOO PASTRY,
APRICOT JAM TURNOVER,
APPLE CHAUSSON

BUTTERMILK
CHOCOLATE CAKE
· · ·

Be careful not to underbake this delicious cake—it's supposed to have a light crumb, not a texture like dense brownies.

4½ ounces (⅞ cup) scant all-purpose flour
¼ teaspoon baking powder
dash salt
1 ounce (¼ cup) unsweetened cocoa powder
7 ounces (¾ cup) generous sugar
2 eggs, large
5 ounces (1¼ sticks) unsalted butter, soft and creamy
6 ounces (¾ cup) buttermilk
½ teaspoon vanilla extract
confectioners' sugar

Preheat oven to 350°F. Butter and flour an 8-inch square cake pan.

Sift flour, baking powder, salt, and cocoa together and place in bowl of electric mixer. Add sugar. Mix with flat beater at slow speed, then add eggs and soft butter. Mix at medium speed until there are no lumps, 2 to 3 minutes. (Scrape the bottom of the bowl with a spatula to make sure.) The batter should be very thick and creamy. Add buttermilk and vanilla and mix until completely blended, but don't overmix or the batter will "break" and collapse. Pour into prepared pan and bake for 45 minutes, until top feels springy to light finger pressure, and a skewer inserted in the center of the cake comes out clean. Unmold upside down and cool on rack. Dust with confectioners' sugar before serving. *Serves 8.*

· · · ◊ · · ·

SAVANNAH LOAF CAKE

. . .

6 ounces (¾ cup) scant sugar
6 ounces (1½ sticks) unsalted butter, soft and creamy
3 eggs, large
2 egg yolks, large
6 ounces (1¼ cups) scant all-purpose flour
1½ teaspoons baking powder
4½ tablespoons sour cream
2 tablespoons dark rum
1½ tablespoons unsweetened cocoa powder

Preheat oven to 350°F. Butter and flour 8-by-4½-inch loaf pan.

In bowl of electric mixer, combine sugar and butter. Beat with paddle until very light and fluffy, then add eggs and egg yolks one at a time, beating well after each addition. Sift flour and baking powder together and pour around edge of bowl. Beat until mixture is light and creamy. Add sour cream and mix well. Remove bowl from mixer.

Using a plastic spatula, fold in rum. Spread half the batter into the prepared cake pan. Sift cocoa into remaining batter and spoon into pan. Using a fork or spatula held upright, cut down to bottom of batter in a continuous S-shaped swirl pattern. This will create a marbled effect in the baked cake. Bake for 45 minutes, until cake is golden and a skewer inserted in the center comes out clean. Unmold and cool on rack. *Serves 8.*

. . . ◊ . . .

WALNUT CAKE
WITH COFFEE SAUCE

· · ·

The coffee sauce makes a wonderful contrast in flavor and texture, but this cake is also delicious plain.

Cake:

4 eggs, large
3 ounces (¾ stick) unsalted butter
8 ounces (2 cups) walnut pieces
5 ounces (⅔ cup) scant sugar
1¾ ounce (⅓ cup) all-purpose flour
¼ teaspoon baking powder
confectioners' sugar

Coffee Sauce:

1 pint (2 cups) heavy cream
1 tablespoon instant espresso coffee powder
4 ounces (½ cup) sugar
2 ounces (½ stick) unsalted butter, soft and creamy

Preheat oven to 350°F. Butter and flour an 8-inch square cake pan.
Separate 3 of the eggs. Melt butter and allow to brown slightly. In bowl of food processor or blender, combine walnuts with 2 tablespoons of the sugar. Process until evenly ground but not oily. Sift flour and baking powder together and set aside.

In bowl of electric mixer, whip the 3 egg whites until foamy and gradually add remaining sugar. Continue beating at medium-high speed until mixture is very stiff and glossy. In a separate bowl, combine ground walnuts, the 3 reserved egg yolks, and the whole egg.

Pour lukewarm butter over mixture, and quickly fold in half the beaten egg whites and then the sifted flour. Rapidly fold in remaining

· ·

egg whites and spoon into prepared cake pan. Bake for 25 to 30 minutes, until cake feels springy to light finger pressure. Unmold upside down onto rack and let cool. Dust with confectioners' sugar, and serve with Coffee Sauce if desired. *Serves 8.*

COFFEE SAUCE: Heat cream to boiling point. In a bowl, combine instant coffee and sugar. Add boiling cream and whisk together. Let cool to room temperature and beat in the butter, little by little. *Makes approximately 2 cups.*

. . . ◇ . . .

FLOURLESS
CHOCOLATE-WALNUT CAKE
. . .

INTERMEDIATE

Ground walnuts take the place of flour in this cake. Be sure they are light and powdery, not ground to a paste.

5 ounces (1¼ stick) unsalted butter
2 ounces (½ cup) unsweetened cocoa powder
5 egg yolks, large
7 ounces (¾ cup) generous sugar
5 egg whites, large
6 ounces (1½ cups) walnut pieces, ground
½ medium lemon, peel only, minced
2 ounces (4 tablespoons) candied orange peel, minced
    (recipe, page 214), or use store-bought variety
confectioners' sugar

Preheat oven to 375°F. Butter an 8-inch square cake pan.
    Melt butter, stir in cocoa, and let cool to lukewarm. Beat egg yolks and *half* the sugar together until thick and very pale in color. In a separate bowl, beat egg whites until soft peaks form. Add remaining

sugar and beat until stiff and glossy. Fold butter-chocolate mixture into the beaten yolks, then fold in half the egg whites. Fold in walnuts, then remaining egg whites, and lemon and orange peel. Pour batter into prepared pan and bake for 25 minutes, until cake feels springy and a skewer inserted in the center comes out clean. Unmold and cool on rack. Dust with confectioners' sugar before serving. *Serves 8.*

· · · ◊ · · ·

F L O U R L E S S
A L M O N D   C A K E
W I T H   F R O Z E N   E G G S
· · ·

INTERMEDIATE

I developed a technique of using chopped frozen raw eggs in this type of flourless cake: the batter stays cold and light even though it is beaten for a long time. (Normally, this would make the nuts become warm and oily, which would result in a liquid batter and a heavy cake.) If you are grinding almonds in a food processor to make almond meal, combine with the sugar to keep the meal dry and aerated.

4 eggs, large
10 ounces (2½ cups) almond meal (page 1)
8 ounces (1 cup) generous sugar
3 ounces (¾ stick) unsalted butter, soft and creamy
1 ounce (¼ cup) cornstarch
½ teaspoon baking powder
confectioners' sugar

Break the eggs onto a sheet cake pan and freeze until solid, about 1 hour.

Preheat oven to 375°F. Butter and flour an 8-inch square cake pan.

Combine almond meal, sugar, and butter in bowl of electric mixer. Beat with paddle until light and creamy. Chop the frozen eggs into small pieces and add to the batter little by little. Beat at medium-high speed until a firm, creamy emulsion is formed, about 5 minutes. Sift cornstarch and baking powder; add to batter. Beat until incorporated but do not overmix and deflate the mixture. Transfer to prepared pan and bake for 20 to 25 minutes, until cake feels springy and a skewer inserted in the center comes out clean. Unmold upside down and let cool on rack. Dust with confectioners' sugar. Serve plain or with fresh berries. *Serves 8.*

· · · ◊ · · ·

FLOURLESS CHOCOLATE-ALMOND CAKE WITH FROZEN EGGS

· · ·

INTERMEDIATE

If grinding almonds and hazelnuts in a food processor to obtain meal, add a little of the sugar called for in the recipe to prevent the ground nuts from turning oily.

4 eggs, large
4 ounces (1 cup) almond meal (page 1)
4 ounces (1 cup) hazelnut meal (page 3)
8 ounces (1 cup) generous sugar
4 ounces (1 stick) unsalted butter, soft
2 ounces (½ cup) unsweetened cocoa powder
1 ounce (¼ cup) cornstarch
½ teaspoon baking powder
confectioners' sugar

Break the eggs onto a sheet cake pan and freeze until solid, about 1 hour.

Preheat oven to 350°F. Butter and flour an 8-inch square cake pan. Combine almond meal, hazelnut meal, sugar, and butter in bowl of electric mixer and beat with paddle until light and creamy. Chop the frozen eggs into small pieces and add to the batter little by little, beating at medium-high speed until well incorporated and a firm emulsion is formed—about 10 minutes. It must be very light and creamy. Sift cocoa, cornstarch, and baking powder together and fold into batter with a plastic spatula. Spread batter into prepared pan and bake for 30 to 35 minutes, until top feels springy and a skewer inserted in the center of the cake comes out clean. Unmold and cool on a rack.

Lay five 1-inch strips of paper diagonally across the cake at equal intervals. Sift confectioners' sugar on top, then carefully remove paper. Serve plain or accompany with fresh berries. *Serves 8.*

· · · ◊ · · ·

8.

Génoise &
Sponge Cake
Variations

. . . ◊ . . .

Génoise, sponge cakes, and ladyfingers all belong to the same family. I use them in one form or another as the foundation for many elaborate desserts. Happily, it is easy to get good results if you remember these tips.

In a true génoise, the eggs and sugar are whisked together in a bowl set over (but not touching!) barely simmering water, until just warm to the touch. It is important not to overheat this smooth emulsion, or your cake will be dry. The mixture is then beaten, off the heat, until it cools. It will treble in volume as it does so, and should form a slowly dissolving ribbon from a lifted beater. However, don't overbeat, or there will be too much air in your mixture and the baked cake will be dry and crumbly.

Always sift your flour first, even if the makers say it is presifted. (I recommend using ordinary unbleached all-purpose flour.) A little baking powder provides added insurance, but do not use too much or your cake will overrise and develop a "holey" texture. Don't drop your sifted flour all at once on top of your defenseless egg and sugar mixture—you will drive the air out. Instead, pour it around the edge of the bowl, and then incorporate it by folding it in by hand. If using melted butter, be sure that it is lukewarm, and pour it around the edge of the bowl before folding it in. Dumping hot butter on top of your batter is a sure way to deflate it.

Other types of sponge cakes are made by simply beating egg yolks and sugar together until thick and light, then folding in the sifted flour and separately beaten egg whites. Always add some of the sugar to your egg whites; they will hold their volume better.

When baking round sponge cakes, bake them the day before they are to be used. This type of cake is rather crumbly when very fresh and will not slice cleanly or absorb flavoring syrups properly. Enclosed in plastic wrap, they will keep for a week in the refrigerator, or for a month in the freezer.

Large sheet cakes and sponge rolls (Biscuits Roulades), on the other hand, should be baked and used immediately so that they don't dry out. When baking in a regular-sized domestic oven, as opposed to a big professional convection oven, it is better to bake one sheet cake at a time. The second cake can wait for 8 to 10 minutes without much harm.

To unmold round or square cakes easily, simply butter your cake pan very thoroughly. There is no need to flour the pan unless you want the cake to have a particularly smooth surface. Always unmold cakes as soon as they are baked and place on a rack to cool; otherwise trapped steam will cause them to collapse and shrink, and get soggy.

Sheet cakes should be unmolded upside down onto a rack, and allowed to rest for 1 minute before peeling off the baking parchment.

One last thing: in professional bakeries, cakes are assembled on cake boards—circles or rectangles of white, moisture-resistant cardboard. It makes it easy to pick the cakes up, and it certainly facilitates decorating the sides! At home you can use any kind of cardboard cut to the right size and covered tightly with tin foil, or you can utilize the base from a loose-bottomed tart pan.

· · · ◇ · · ·

Index:

· · · ◇ · · ·

Génoise &
Sponge Cake
Variations

Traditional Génoise Sponge Cake (Round)
Rich Génoise Sponge Cake (Round)
Chocolate-Almond Génoise Sponge Cake (Round)
Traditional Sponge Roll—Biscuit Roulade (Sheet Cake)
Chocolate Sponge Roll (Sheet Cake)
Traditional Almond Sponge (Sheet Cake)
Hazelnut-Almond Meringue (Sheet Cake)
Rich Chocolate Sponge (Sheet Cake)
Rich Chocolate-Almond Sponge (Sheet Cake)
Coffee Génoise (Sheet Cake)
Ladyfingers
Chocolate Ladyfingers

TRADITIONAL
GÉNOISE SPONGE CAKE
(Round)

. . .

INTERMEDIATE

This classic preparation is used as the basis for many different elaborate cakes, such as my Sun Valley Cake (recipe, page 139). If it is to be sliced in layers and filled, as opposed to being eaten plain with just a dusting of confectioners' sugar, I recommend that you bake it the day before it is to be used. It will cut more cleanly.

3 eggs, large
2¼ ounces (¼ cup) generous sugar
2¼ ounces (½ cup) all-purpose flour
½ teaspoon baking powder

Preheat oven to 350°F. Grease a 9-inch-diameter cake pan generously with butter so that the baked cake will unmold easily. It is not necessary to flour the pan.

Place eggs in bowl of electric mixer and pour sugar on top, beating vigorously by hand with a wire whisk. Set the bowl over a pan of simmering water; the water must not touch the bottom of the bowl. Whisk until the egg-sugar mixture is warm to the touch, at 100°F. Remove bowl from heat and place on mixer stand. Beat mixture well with wire whip at medium speed until it cools and forms a complete emulsion, about 10 minutes. The batter should increase greatly in volume and become very pale in color, and fall from a spatula in a slowly dissolving ribbon. Remove bowl from stand.

Sift flour and baking powder together and fold into batter by hand. Pour batter into prepared pan. Bake for 25 minutes, until cake is golden and feels springy to a light finger touch. Unmold onto rack and let cool. *Makes one 9-inch cake.*

RICH
GÉNOISE SPONGE CAKE
(Round)

· · ·

INTERMEDIATE

Like the Traditional Génoise Sponge Cake, this cake can be served plain with a dusting of confectioners' sugar, but is used mainly as the base for many different gâteaux, including my Princess Cake (recipe, page 141). I recommend that you bake it the day before an elaborate layer cake is to be assembled, as it will slice better.

3 eggs, large
2½ ounces (5 tablespoons) sugar
2½ ounces (⅓ cup) all-purpose flour
½ teaspoon baking powder
½ ounce (1 tablespoon) unsalted butter, melted and cooled to lukewarm

Preheat oven to 350°F. Grease a 9-inch-diameter cake pan generously with butter so that the baked cake will unmold easily. It is not necessary to flour the pan.

Place eggs in bowl of electric mixer and pour sugar on top, beating vigorously by hand with a wire whisk. Set the bowl over a pan of simmering water; the water must not touch the bottom of the bowl. Whisk until the egg-sugar mixture is warm to the touch, at 100°F. Remove bowl from heat and place on stand. Beat mixture well with wire whip at medium speed until it cools and forms a complete emulsion, about 10 minutes. The batter should increase greatly in volume and become very pale in color, and will fall from a spatula in a slowly dissolving ribbon. Remove bowl from stand.

Sift flour and baking powder together and fold into batter by hand. Fold in lukewarm butter, mixing only until incorporated. Pour batter into prepared pan. Bake for 25 minutes, until cake is golden and feels springy to a light finger touch. Unmold onto rack and let cool. *Makes one 9-inch cake.*

· · · ◇ · · ·

CHOCOLATE-ALMOND
GÉNOISE SPONGE CAKE
(Round)

· · ·

INTERMEDIATE

If this cake is being used as a base for the Valencia Cake (recipe, page 143), it is best to bake it the day before the cake is to be sliced and assembled. It will slice more cleanly, without crumbs. Alternatively, it can be baked and served as soon as it is cool, plain or with confectioners' sugar on top.

5 eggs, large
5 ounces (⅔ cup) scant sugar
3½ ounces (½ cup) scant all-purpose flour
1½ ounces (6 tablespoons) unsweetened cocoa powder
1½ ounces (⅓ cup) almond meal (page 1)
½ teaspoon baking powder

Preheat oven to 350°F. Grease a 9-inch-diameter cake pan generously with butter so that the baked cake will unmold easily. It is not necessary to flour the pan unless you are serving it plain and want a very smooth surface.

Place eggs in bowl of electric mixer and pour sugar on top, beating vigorously by hand with a wire whisk. Set the bowl over a pan of simmering water; the water must not touch the bottom of the bowl.

Whisk until the egg-sugar mixture is warm to the touch, at 100°F. Remove bowl from heat and place on mixer stand. Beat mixture well with wire whip at medium speed until it cools and forms a complete emulsion, about 10 minutes. The batter should increase greatly in volume and become very pale in color, and will fall from a spatula in a slowly dissolving ribbon. Remove bowl from stand.

Sift flour, cocoa, almond meal, and baking powder together and fold into batter. Spoon into prepared pan. Bake for 25 minutes, until cake feels springy to a light finger touch. Unmold onto rack and let cool. *Makes one 9-inch cake.*

· · · ◊ · · ·

TRADITIONAL SPONGE ROLL — BISCUIT ROULADE

(Sheet Cake)

· · ·

INTERMEDIATE

The French call this a sponge roll, as its springy texture permits rolling up with a jam or cream filling. I also use it for layering with jam to make striped cakes, such as the Melody Cake (recipe, page 146) and the Strawberry Pinstripe Cake (recipe, page 148).

9 egg whites, large
9 ounces (1 cup plus 2 tablespoons) sugar
5 egg yolks, large
1 whole egg, large
8 ounces (1½ cups) all-purpose flour
½ teaspoon baking powder

Preheat oven to 425°F. Line two 17-by-12-by-1-inch sheet cake pans with baking parchment, securing the paper with a dab of butter at each corner.

Place egg whites in a bowl and whisk until soft peaks form. Slowly add 2 ounces of the sugar and continue whisking until stiff and glossy. Place yolks, the remaining 7 ounces of sugar, and the whole egg in a separate bowl and beat at high speed until light and lemon-colored. Sift flour and baking powder together onto a sheet of wax paper. Fold half the egg whites into the sugar-yolks emulsion, then fold in flour. Fold in remaining egg whites. Spread batter evenly into prepared pans. Bake for 8 to 10 minutes, until golden and springy to the touch. Unmold onto racks, peel off paper after 1 minute, and let cool. *Makes two 17-by-12-inch sheet cakes.*

. . . ◊ . . .

CHOCOLATE SPONGE ROLL

(Sheet Cake)

. . .

Certain cakes, such as the Pineapple Crown Cake (recipe, page 152), require two sponge sheets, plain and chocolate. Proceed as above, and fill the first sheet cake pan with half the batter. To the remaining mixture add ¾ ounce (3 tablespoons) of sifted cocoa powder. Fill the second pan with this chocolate batter and bake as usual.

. . . ◊ . . .

TRADITIONAL
ALMOND SPONGE
(Sheet Cake)

. . .

INTERMEDIATE

I use this sheet cake as a base for the sumptuous Opéra Cake (recipe, page 155), though of course you can use many other types of fillings and glazes. In this cake, the egg whites must be beaten separately. To save time, beat them first in an electric mixer and transfer to another bowl. Then beat the whole eggs in the mixer bowl; there is no need to wash it or the whip.

4 egg whites, large
3 ounces (⅓ cup) generous sugar
2 ounces (½ cup) almond meal (page 1)
2 ounces (½ cup) scant all-purpose flour
½ teaspoon baking powder
2 whole eggs, large

Preheat oven to 400°F. Line a 17-by-12-by-1-inch sheet cake pan with baking parchment.

In bowl of electric mixer, whip egg whites until soft peaks start to form. Slowly add *half* the sugar and whip until mixture is stiff and glossy. Transfer to another bowl. Sift the almond meal, flour, and baking powder together onto a sheet of wax paper.

Add whole eggs and remaining sugar to mixer bowl. Whip until thick and lemon-colored. Remove bowl from stand.

Fold half the egg whites into the egg-sugar mixture. Fold in almond-flour mixture. Fold in remaining egg whites. Spread batter evenly into prepared pan. Bake for 8 to 10 minutes, until cake feels springy. Unmold onto rack, peel off paper after 1 minute, and let cool. *Makes one 17-by-12-inch sheet cake.*

. . . ◊ . . .

HAZELNUT-ALMOND
MERINGUE

(Sheet Cake)

. . .

INTERMEDIATE

This sheet cake, which is somewhere between a soft nut meringue and a sponge cake, forms the base for my Charlenoit Cake (recipe, page 158), a very special creation filled with chocolate buttercream and praliné custard cream.

3 ounces (¾ cup) hazelnuts
3 ounces (¾ cup) almonds
¾ ounce (3 tablespoons) all-purpose flour
5 egg whites, large
6½ ounces (¾ cup) sugar

Preheat oven to 350°F. Spread hazelnuts and almonds on a baking sheet and toast until lightly browned, about 15 minutes. Let cool. It is unnecessary to remove the skins. Grind with the flour (to help prevent nuts from becoming oily) in food processor or blender.

Increase oven heat to 475°F. Line a 17-by-12-by-1-inch sheet cake pan with baking parchment.

Whip egg whites until soft peaks start to form. Slowly add *half* the sugar and continue beating until stiff and glossy. Combine remaining sugar with ground nuts and flour. Stir in one-quarter of the egg whites. Fold in remaining egg whites, being careful not to deflate the batter. Spread evenly into prepared pan. Bake for 8 to 10 minutes, until cake feels springy. Unmold onto rack, peel off paper after 1 minute, and let cool. *Makes one 17-by-12-inch sheet cake.*

. . . ◇ . . .

RICH CHOCOLATE SPONGE

(Sheet Cake)

. . .

INTERMEDIATE

I employ this moist chocolate sponge cake for the Lippizaner Cake (recipe, page 161) and the Grand Marnier Soufflé Cake (recipe, page 164).

8 egg whites, large
6½ ounces (¾ cup) sugar
4 ounces (¾ cup) scant all-purpose flour
½ teaspoon baking powder
2 ounces (½ cup) unsweetened cocoa powder
8 egg yolks, large
1 ounce (¼ stick) unsalted butter, melted and cooled
 to lukewarm

Preheat oven to 425°F. Line a 17-by-12-by-1-inch sheet cake pan with baking parchment.

In bowl of electric mixer, whip egg whites until soft peaks start to form. Slowly add *one-third* of the sugar and whip until mixture is stiff and glossy. Transfer to another bowl. Sift flour, baking powder, and cocoa together onto a sheet of wax paper.

Add egg yolks and remaining sugar to mixer bowl. Whip until light and lemon-colored. Remove bowl from mixer stand.

Fold half the egg whites into the egg-sugar mixture. Fold in the flour-cocoa mixture. Fold in remaining egg whites. Pour lukewarm butter around edge of bowl and quickly incorporate, being careful not to deflate the batter. Spread evenly into prepared pan. Bake for 8 to 10 minutes, until cake feels springy to the touch. Unmold onto rack, peel off paper after 1 minute, and let cool. *Makes one 17-by-12-inch sheet cake.*

RICH CHOCOLATE-ALMOND SPONGE

(Sheet Cake)

. . .

I use this chocolate sheet cake for my Washington Cake (recipe, page 166) and the Arlequin Cake (recipe, page 168), among others.

7 eggs, large
7 ounces (¾ cup) generous sugar
6 ounces (1¼ cup) scant all-purpose flour
3 ounces (¾ cup) unsweetened cocoa powder
1½ ounce (⅓ cup) almond meal (page 1)
½ teaspoon baking powder
2 ounces (½ stick) unsalted butter, melted and cooled
    to lukewarm

Preheat oven to 400°F. Line a 17-by-12-by-1-inch sheet cake pan with baking parchment.

Place eggs in bowl of electric mixer and pour sugar on top, beating vigorously by hand with a wire whisk. Set the bowl over a pan of simmering water; the water must not touch the bottom of the bowl. Whisk until the egg-sugar mixture is warm to the touch, at 100°F. Remove bowl from heat and place on mixer stand. Beat mixture well with wire whip at medium speed until it cools and forms a complete emulsion, about 10 minutes. The batter should increase greatly in volume and become very pale in color, and will fall from a spatula in a slowly dissolving ribbon. Remove bowl from stand.

Sift the flour, cocoa, almond meal, and baking powder together onto a sheet of wax paper. Fold lightly into batter. Pour the lukewarm butter around edge of bowl and quickly fold in. Spread batter evenly into prepared pan. Bake for 8 to 10 minutes, until cake feels springy to the touch. Unmold onto rack, peel off paper after 1 minute, and let cool. *Makes one 17-by-12-inch sheet cake.*

. . . .

COFFEE GÉNOISE

(Sheet Cake)

. . .

INTERMEDIATE

This sheet cake is used in the Jester Cake (recipe, page 170) and, of course, is good layered with coffee or chocolate-flavored buttercream.

5 eggs, large
5 ounces (⅔ cup) scant sugar
1 ounce (¼ stick) unsalted butter
1 tablespoon instant espresso coffee powder
1 tablespoon boiling water
5 ounces (1 cup) scant all-purpose flour
½ teaspoon baking powder

Preheat oven to 400°F. Line a 17-by-12-by-1-inch sheet cake pan with baking parchment.

Place eggs in bowl of electric mixer and pour sugar on top, beating vigorously with a wire whisk. Set the bowl over a pan of simmering water; the water must not touch the bottom of the bowl. Whisk until the egg-sugar mixture is warm to the touch, at 100°F. Remove bowl from heat and place on mixer stand. Beat mixture well with wire whip at medium speed until it cools and forms a complete emulsion, about 10 minutes. The batter should increase greatly in volume and become very pale in color, and will fall from a spatula in a slowly dissolving ribbon. Remove bowl from stand.

Melt the butter in a small saucepan. Dissolve the espresso coffee powder in 1 tablespoon boiling water and add to butter. Cool to lukewarm by placing pan in cold water. Sift the flour and baking powder together and fold into batter. Pour the butter-coffee mixture around the edge of bowl and quickly fold in. Spread batter evenly into prepared pan. Bake for 8 to 10 minutes, until cake feels springy to the touch. Unmold onto rack, peel off paper after 1 minute, and let cool. *Makes one 17-by-12-inch sheet cake.*

· · · ◊ · · ·

L A D Y F I N G E R S
· · ·

INTERMEDIATE

These soft sponge fingers can be served alone or with fruit, frozen desserts, and custards. When using them to line a mold for a charlotte, I pipe them close together so that they form a continuous band.

4 egg whites, large
5½ ounces (⅔ cup) sugar
4 egg yolks, large
4½ ounces (⅞ cup) scant all-purpose flour
½ teaspoon baking powder
confectioners' sugar

Preheat oven to 400°F. Line two 17-inch-by-12-by-1-inch baking sheets with baking parchment. Fit a large pastry bag with a plain ½-inch round tube.

Place egg whites in bowl of electric mixer and whip until soft peaks start to form. Slowly add 2 tablespoons of the sugar and continue beating until stiff and glossy. Transfer to another bowl. Add yolks to mixer bowl and stir in remaining sugar. Whip until thick and very pale in color and remove bowl from stand.

Sift flour and baking powder together onto a sheet of wax paper. Fold half the egg whites into the egg-yolk mixture. Fold in the flour, and then fold in the remaining egg whites. Transfer mixture to pastry bag and pipe out 2-inch-long fingers onto prepared baking sheet. Sift a layer of confectioners' sugar on top. Pick up the baking parchment by two corners and let the excess sugar fall off—the ladyfingers will remain in place. Bake for 8 minutes. *Makes approximately 60.*

. . . ◊ . . .

CHOCOLATE LADYFINGERS

Proceed as above, but substitute 4 ounces (scant ³/₄ cup) flour plus ¹/₂ ounce (2 tablespoons) unsweetened cocoa powder for the plain flour.

. . . ◊ . . .

9.

Gâteaux

$$\cdots \diamond \cdots$$

Although the cakes and desserts in this chapter appear—and in fact are—impressive, they are relatively simple to assemble. In most cases, layers of sponge cake or génoise are cut from a sheet cake. These are saturated with liqueur-flavored Simple Syrup and sandwiched together with buttercream or mousse. The cake is well chilled to facilitate handling, and finished with more buttercream or a glaze. Simple, elegant decorations such as chocolate leaves and marzipan acorns add a professional touch.

The main thing to remember when assembling your cake is to have your cake layers absolutely even in thickness. Trim them if necessary. (Save and freeze cake trimmings; they can be put to good use in desserts such as a Diplomat—recipe, page 163.) Keep your layers of cake and filling even and regular. Where appropriate, trim the edges with a hot knife blade, after first chilling the cake, to show off the interior. Always use a cake board cut to the appropriate size under your cakes—this makes it simple to pick them up from underneath. If you cannot obtain professional moisture-resistant cardboard cake boards, make your own with ordinary cardboard covered tightly with aluminum foil. Finally, when serving your creations, be sure to let them stand at room temperature for a few minutes so that the flavors can develop. Like good wines, they should not be served so cold that they cannot be tasted fully.

Index:

· · · ◇ · · ·

Gâteaux

SUN VALLEY CAKE

. . .

I named this delicate cake for the famous Idaho ski resort. First, a traditional génoise is split and moistened with lemon-vodka syrup. The cake is then filled with a lemon mousse that is as light as snow, and topped with fresh raspberries. The sides are covered with whipped cream. Like all professional chefs, I use a cake ring (see illustration on page 6) to support the mousse as it sets up. If necessary, you can substitute the rim from a 9-inch springform pan. I recommend that you bake the génoise the day before the cake is to be assembled, as it will slice better.

Cake:

Traditional Génoise Sponge (recipe, page 125)

Lemon Syrup:

5 ounces (⅝ cup) Simple Syrup (recipe page 237)
2 ounces (¼ cup) lemon juice
1 tablespoon vodka

Lemon Mousse:

10 ounces (1¼ cups) whipping cream
¼ ounce (1 envelope) unflavored gelatin
2 tablespoons cold water
2 ounces (¼ cup) lemon juice
2 ounces (¼ cup) generous sugar
2 egg yolks, large
8 ounces (1 cup) sour cream

Decoration:

8 ounces (1 cup) whipping cream
4 ounces (½ cup) raspberry jam
12 ounces (2 baskets) fresh raspberries
confectioners' sugar

TO PREPARE LEMON SYRUP: Combine Simple Syrup with lemon juice and vodka and stir well.

TO PREPARE LEMON MOUSSE: Beat cream to soft peaks and refrigerate. Soften gelatin in 1 tablespoon cold water. Heat lemon juice in a small pan, add gelatin, and whisk for a few seconds. Combine sugar with 1 tablespoon water in an unlined copper sugar pan or a small stainless steel saucepan. Cook over medium-high heat to the soft ball stage, 240° F. While sugar is heating, place egg yolks in bowl and beat lightly. When sugar is ready, pour it slowly over egg yolks, whisking vigorously at the same time. Add the lemon juice–gelatin mixture and continue beating until mixture is cold. Gradually beat in sour cream, a spoonful at a time. Beat at low speed until creamy and lump free. Fold in the whipped cream.

TO ASSEMBLE CAKE: Place a cake ring or springform pan rim on a baking sheet lined with parchment paper. Slice the génoise into two even layers and place one in the cake ring. Using a large pastry brush, soak with lemon syrup. Pour in the lemon cream filling and top with the second cake layer. Brush with lemon syrup and place cake in the freezer for 3 to 4 hours.

TO DECORATE: Whip cream and refrigerate. Remove cake from freezer, run a sharp knife around edges, and remove cake ring. Set the cake on a cake board or circle of cardboard covered with tin foil. Spread top of cake with raspberry jam and cover with fresh raspberries. Transfer whipped cream to pastry bag fitted with a plain ½-inch round tip and cover top edge and sides of cake with cream. Smooth the sides with a long baker's spatula. Let cake thaw in refrigerator for 2 hours. Allow cake to stand at room temperature for 15 minutes and dust raspberries lightly with confectioners' sugar before serving.

Sun Valley Cake will keep for a maximum of two days under refrigeration. *Serves 8.*

PRINCESS CAKE

. . .

I believe that this delicate, dome-shaped cake originated in Sweden. In my version, three layers of buttery génoise are soaked with gin-raspberry syrup and filled with a smooth custard cream. A thin layer of pale green marzipan cloaks the outside, and it is topped with a rose, either of marzipan or a real one. I recommend that you bake the génoise the day before the cake is to be assembled, as it will slice better.

Cake:

Rich Génoise Sponge (recipe, page 126)

Raspberry Syrup:

5 ounces (⅝ cup) Simple Syrup (recipe, page 237)
4 ounces (½ cup) raspberry jam
1 tablespoon English gin

Custard Cream Filling:

8 ounces (1 cup) generous sugar
8 eggs, large
2 ounces (½ cup) scant all-purpose flour
1 pint (2 cups) milk
1 tablespoon English gin
8 ounces (2 sticks) unsalted butter, soft

Decoration:

12 ounces tinted pale green marzipan (recipe, page 243)
confectioners' sugar
bittersweet chocolate, melted, for piping scroll
1 pink marzipan rose (recipe, page 245)
2 green marzipan leaves (recipe, page 246)

TO PREPARE RASPBERRY SYRUP: Place Simple Syrup in blender or food processor with raspberry jam and gin. Blend until smooth.

TO MAKE CUSTARD CREAM: Place sugar and eggs in a bowl and beat until pale and thick. Beat in sifted flour. Heat milk to boiling and pour a little into the egg mixture. Stir quickly and pour the combined mixture back into the saucepan. Whisk vigorously until custard boils and thickens, and turns shiny. Pour custard into a clean bowl and lightly "paint" the top surface with a piece of cold butter. This will prevent the custard from forming a skin as it cools. When custard is cold, stir in the gin. Cut soft butter into small pieces and add to custard a little at a time, beating at low speed. Beat at high speed for 1 minute, until cream is very light and airy.

TO ASSEMBLE CAKE: Cut génoise into three equal layers. Put bottom layer on a cake board or on an 8½-inch circle of cardboard covered with tin foil. Saturate cake layer with raspberry syrup. Cover with about one-quarter of the custard cream, mounding it up slightly in the center, as the finished cake is dome-shaped. Cover with second layer of cake, soak with syrup as before, and mound with custard cream. Top with third layer of cake and soak with syrup. Cover sides and top of cake with the remaining custard cream, mounding it smoothly. Set cake in freezer for 60 minutes.

TO DECORATE: Roll marzipan into a ⅛-inch thick circle about 14 inches in diameter. Do this on a marble slab or between two sheets of plastic wrap. Place over cake, smoothing it closely against top and sides. Trim off excess at base. (Save trimmings for marzipan leaves, etc.) Place a 5-inch-diameter circle of cardboard on top of cake. Sift confectioners' sugar over it so that a light drift of sugar falls down the sides. Remove cardboard. Place melted chocolate in a small paper cone and pipe a fine scroll on top of cake. Top with a pale pink marzipan rose and two green marzipan leaves, securing them with a little chocolate. Refrigerate cake until required. Let cake stand at room temperature for 15 minutes before serving.

For a simpler presentation, omit the chocolate scroll, marzipan rose, and leaves and use a small fresh rose instead, placing it on the cake just before serving.

The Princess Cake will keep well for two or three days in the refrigerator. *Serves 8.*

· · · ◇ · · ·

VALENCIA CAKE
· · ·

ADVANCED

The Spanish introduced chocolate to Europe in the sixteenth century, and Valencia was famous for her oranges long before that, so my chocolate-orange Valencia Cake has a very long history! You will need a cake ring or the rim from a 9-inch springform pan to support this very light cake as it sets up. I recommend that you bake the sponge cake the day before the cake is to be assembled.

Cake:

Chocolate-Almond Génoise Sponge (recipe, page 127)

Orange Syrup:

5 ounces (⅝ cup) Simple Syrup (recipe, page 237)
5 ounces (⅝ cup) frozen orange juice concentrate, thawed
2 ounces (¼ cup) vodka

Orange Cream:

5½ ounces (1 stick plus 3 tablespoons) unsalted butter, soft
½ ounce (4 teaspoons) unflavored gelatin
1 tablespoon cold water
4 ounces (½ cup) milk
5 ounces (⅝ cup) frozen orange juice concentrate, thawed
16 ounces (2 cups) heavy cream

Decoration:

1 orange
16 ounces (2 cups) Simple Syrup (recipe, page 237)
4 ounces bittersweet chocolate

TO PREPARE THE ORANGE SYRUP: Blend Simple Syrup with the orange juice concentrate and vodka.

TO MAKE THE ORANGE CREAM: Place butter in bowl and beat until creamy. Soak gelatin in cold water for 5 minutes. Place milk and orange juice concentrate in a saucepan and bring to a boil. Add gelatin and butter to milk, stirring until blended. Transfer to a bowl and let cool to 85°F. In a separate bowl, whip cream until soft peaks form. Add to buttermilk mixture and blend well but do not overmix.

TO ASSEMBLE CAKE: Place a 9-inch cake ring on a cake board. Slice sponge into 2 even layers and place one in the cake ring. Using a brush, saturate cake with orange syrup. Top with second cake layer and saturate with syrup. (The cake must be well soaked, so it is advisable to split it first.) Pour orange cream over cake to top of cake ring, smoothing the surface with a spatula. Freeze for 3 to 4 hours.

TO DECORATE: Remove peel from a thin-skinned orange and cut into ⅛-by-2-inch strips. Place in a saucepan, cover with cold water, bring to a boil, and drain. Repeat this step twice more, to remove bitterness. Combine drained peel with Simple Syrup and let simmer for 45 minutes. Let cool in the syrup.

Melt chocolate in a small bowl over hot water. Line a baking sheet with parchment paper (or tin foil) and spread chocolate out in a very thin layer. Refrigerate until chocolate hardens, about 10 minutes. Break chocolate into irregular triangles or shards about 2 inches across.

Remove cake from freezer, run a sharp knife around the edges, and lift off the cake ring. Spread candied orange peel and a little of the reduced orange syrup on top of the cake. Brush sides with orange syrup and decorate with shards of chocolate, placing them as close together as possible. (See illustration.) Let cake thaw in refrigerator for 2 hours, and stand at room temperature for 15 minutes before serving.

The Valencia Cake will keep for two days in the refrigerator. *Serves 8.*

· · ◇ · ·

MELODY CAKE

. . .

This spectacular summer dessert is made by lining a 1-quart metal half-sphere bowl with thinly sliced jelly roll and filling the center with raspberry bavarois. The unmolded cake is glazed and served with a fresh raspberry sauce.

Cake:

Traditional Sponge Roll (2 sheet cakes) (recipe, page 128)

Jam Filling for Cake:

1 pound (2 cups) raspberry jam

Cointreau Syrup:

5 ounces (⅝ cup) Simple Syrup (recipe, page 237) combined
  with
5 ounces (⅝ cup) Cointreau

Raspberry Bavarois:

1 pint (2 cups) milk
½ ounce (2 envelopes) unflavored gelatin
1 tablespoon cold water
6 egg yolks, large
4 ounces (½ cup) sugar
4 tablespoons Cointreau
1 pint (2 cups) heavy cream
12 ounces (2 baskets) fresh raspberries

Decoration:

4 ounces (½ cup) Apricot Glaze (recipe, page 241), heated
3 Chocolate Leaves (recipe, page 243)

Raspberry Sauce:

12 ounces (2 baskets) fresh raspberries
6 ounces (¾ cup) Simple Syrup

Bake sponge roll according to the recipe, and as soon as the cakes have cooled, spread with a thin layer of raspberry jam. Roll each one tightly, starting at the long side. Wrap in plastic wrap or tin foil and place in freezer for 1 to 2 hours.

TO MAKE BAVAROIS: Place milk in a saucepan and bring to a boil. Soak gelatin in cold water for 5 minutes. In the meantime, beat yolks and sugar together until light and lemon-colored. Whisk in ½ cup of the boiling milk and then return entire mixture to saucepan. Do not allow to boil again or the egg yolks will become grainy. Whisk constantly over moderate heat until mixture thickens, about 5 minutes. It should coat a spoon lightly and register 160°–165° F. on a candy thermometer. Pour a little of the hot custard over the gelatin, then return entire mixture to saucepan and whisk for a few seconds. Remove from heat, let cool, and add Cointreau. Before mixture sets, whip cream to soft peaks and lightly fold into custard. Carefully fold in raspberries without crushing the fruit.

TO ASSEMBLE: Remove rolled cakes from freezer and cut into ¼-inch slices. Spread slices out on work surface and brush with Cointreau syrup. Starting at the center of a 1-quart half-sphere metal bowl and working outward, line with "roulés," or round slices of cake, fitting them as close together as possible. Fill any little gaps with scraps of cake. Trim top edges even with rim of bowl. Fill mold with bavarois mixture to within ½ inch of top. Cover completely with a double layer of cake slices and trimmings; there must be no gaps. Place in freezer for 3 to 4 hours.

TO DECORATE: Remove cake from freezer, dip bowl in boiling water, wipe dry, and unmold cake. Brush with warm Apricot Glaze and arrange Chocolate Leaves on top. Leave cake in refrigerator for at least 2 hours so that it can thaw, and let stand at room temperature for 15 minutes before serving.

TO MAKE RASPBERRY SAUCE: Place raspberries and Simple Syrup in a blender or food processor, and purée. Pass through a sieve and transfer to a serving bowl or sauceboat. Serve with the Melody Cake. This dessert will keep for two days in the refrigerator. *Serves 8.*

. . . ◇ . . .

S T R A W B E R R Y
P I N S T R I P E   C A K E
. . .

A D V A N C E D

The secret to constructing this elegant cake is that several sheets of génoise are sandwiched together with jam and then thinly sliced. These slices of "striped" cake are used to make a shell, which is filled with a fresh strawberry soufflé. The unmolded cake is lightly glazed, and topped with chocolate-dipped strawberries.

Cake:

Traditional Sponge Roll (2 sheet cakes) (recipe, page 128)

Jam Filling:

1 pound (2 cups) strawberry jam

Strawberry Soufflé:

4½ ounces (½ cup) generous heavy cream
3 ounces (¾ stick) unsalted butter, soft
3 ounces (¾ cup) confectioners' sugar
8 ounces (¾ basket) ripe strawberries
¼ ounce (2 teaspoons) unflavored gelatin
1 tablespoon cold water
2 egg whites, large
2 tablespoons sugar

Syrup:

5 ounces (⅝ cup) Simple Syrup (recipe, page 237),
    combined with
5 ounces (⅝ cup) Kirsch

Decoration:

2 ounces bittersweet chocolate, melted
3 large strawberries, unhulled
4 ounces (½ cup) Apricot Glaze (recipe, page 241)

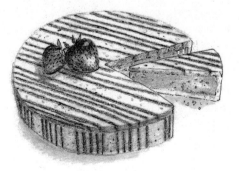

Bake sheet cakes according to the recipe and let cool.

TO PREPARE CAKE SLICES: Puree the jam filling in a blender or food processor to smooth out any whole fruit. Spread one sheet cake with a thin layer of strawberry jam and top with second cake. Cut in half and sandwich cakes together with jam. Repeat this procedure once more. You should now have an 11-by-4½-inch cake with 8 layers. Place cake in freezer for 1 hour, as this will make it easier to slice.

TO PREPARE STRAWBERRY SOUFFLÉ: Using electric mixer, whip cream to soft peaks; transfer to a clean bowl and refrigerate. Beat butter with confectioners' sugar until light and creamy and transfer to a large bowl. Wash and hull strawberries, place in blender or food processor, and purée. Soften gelatin in cold water for 5 minutes. Heat the strawberry purée with the Simple Syrup to simmering point and stir in the gelatin. Combine with the creamed butter and confectioners' sugar. Beat egg whites to firm peaks and slowly beat in sugar. Continue beating until stiff and glossy. Fold egg whites into butter-purée mixture, and then lightly fold in the cream. Refrigerate while making striped cake shell but do not allow to set.

TO ASSEMBLE CAKE: Remove stacked cake from freezer and, starting from one of the long sides, cut into ¼-inch slices. Lay these out on your work surface and push them together. Using a cake pan as a guide, cut out two 8½-inch circles. Cut remaining cake into 2-inch-wide strips, with the stripes of jam running vertically, not horizontally.

Place a 9-inch cake ring on a cake board or a circle of cardboard covered with foil. (Or use rim from a springform pan.) Line sides with strips of vertically striped cake and place one of the cake circles in the bottom. Using a large pastry brush, moisten liberally with Kirsch syrup. Cut remaining scraps of cake into ½-inch cubes. Fill pan one-half full with strawberry soufflé mixture and cover with a layer of cake cubes. Fill with remaining strawberry soufflé until within ¼ inch of top. Cover with second circle of cake and soak with Kirsch syrup. Place in freezer for 2 hours.

TO MAKE DECORATION: Cut the chocolate into small pieces, place in a small bowl, and melt over hot water. Wash and dry the strawberries and half-dip in melted chocolate. Place dipped strawberries on aluminum foil and refrigerate until chocolate hardens.

Remove cake from freezer and run a sharp knife around sides. Reverse onto a plate and remove cake ring and cake board. Brush top and sides of cake with warm Apricot Glaze. Arrange chocolate-dipped strawberries on top, and refrigerate cake for at least 2 hours so that it can thaw. Let stand at room temperature for 15 minutes before serving.

The Strawberry Pinstripe Cake will keep for three to four days in the refrigerator. *Serves 8.*

· · · ◇ · · ·

PINEAPPLE CROWN CAKE

. . .

I created this cake for a pastry exhibition that took place in Paris a few years ago. It won first place for flavor and originality. The cake is composed of Sponge Roll sheet cake in two flavors, moistened with pineapple syrup and filled with custard, pineapple, and sliced banana. The top is covered with glazed sliced bananas and crowned with chocolate "pineapple leaves." You will need a cake ring to support the sides as the cake sets up—or use the rim from a springform pan.

Cake:

Traditional Sponge Roll sheet and Chocolate Sponge Roll sheet,
   one of each (recipe, pages 128 and 129)
1 tablespoon unsalted butter, softened
1 tablespoon confectioners' sugar

Fruit Filling, Decoration, Syrup, and Glaze:

1 ripe pineapple with leafy top
16 ounces (2 cups) generous sugar
2 cups water
2 tablespoons dark rum
3 medium bananas
1 small lemon, juice only
4 ounces (½ cup) Apricot Glaze (recipe, page 241)
4 ounces bittersweet chocolate, melted

Custard Cream:

1 pint (2 cups) milk
4 ounces (½ cup) sugar
4 egg yolks, large
1 ounce (¼ cup) scant all-purpose flour

1 tablespoon rum

1 tablespoon Grand Marnier

5 ounces (⅝ cup) heavy cream, whipped

Prepare chocolate and plain sheet cakes according to the recipe. Let cool. Beat the soft butter with the confectioners' sugar and set aside. (This simple buttercream is for securing the alternating cubes of cake around the sides.)

Peel and core pineapple, reserving the leafy top. Cut fruit into ½-inch-thick slices. In a large pan, combine sugar with water and let boil for 5 minutes to make a Simple Syrup. Add pineapple and let simmer for 10 minutes, or until tender. (Fruit should be covered with Simple Syrup; if not, make more in equal proportions of sugar and water.) Let cool. Remove 1 cup of the pineapple-flavored syrup to a small bowl and stir in 2 tablespoons rum. Set bananas, lemon, and Apricot Glaze aside for later use.

Pull off 12 or 14 of the best-shaped pineapple leaves. Wash and dry carefully. Coat the inside of each leaf with melted chocolate, leaving about 1 inch of leaf showing at the base, and letting it drip off the pointed end. Set leaves on a baking sheet covered with aluminum foil and refrigerate until chocolate sets.

TO MAKE CUSTARD CREAM FILLING: Place milk in a saucepan and heat to boiling. In the meantime, place sugar and egg yolks in a bowl and whisk until pale and thick. Beat in the sifted flour. Pour half the boiling milk into this mixture. Stir quickly and pour the combined mixture back into the saucepan. Whisk vigorously over low-to-medium heat until custard boils and thickens and turns "shiny." Dust with confectioners' sugar to prevent a skin from forming and let cool to room temperature. Stir in the rum and Grand Marnier, and fold in the whipped cream.

TO ASSEMBLE CAKE: Have ready a 9-inch-diameter by 2½-inch-high cake ring, set on a round cardboard cake board.

Cut off four 12-by-3-inch strips of sheet cake, two of each color. It is important that these be of an even thickness; trim if necessary. Lay a dark and a light strip on top of each other and cut into 1-by-1½-inch bricks. Spread the two remaining strips of cake with the reserved buttercream and arrange the little bricks on top, as tightly together as possible, alternating the colors. Press down lightly to make sure they stick. Place one of these double-thickness strips of cake inside the cake ring, bricks facing outward. Add the second strip, trimming to the right size so that it fits snugly. Push the remaining slices of sponge roll together and cut out two 8-inch circles. Place one of these circles inside the cake ring. Brush base and sides liberally with reserved pineapple-rum syrup. Slice one of the bananas and scatter over the cake base. Chop one of the poached pineapple rings and add to sliced banana. Top fruit with half the custard cream filling. Cover the custard with the second circle of sponge cake and moisten well with pineapple-rum syrup. Fill cake with remaining custard cream and smooth the top. Freeze for 1 hour.

TO DECORATE: Loosen the chocolate from the pineapple leaves by inserting a knife tip under the chocolate at the base. They should pop free easily. Remove cake from freezer and run a sharp knife around sides. Take off cake ring. Slice remaining 2 bananas and arrange, overlapping, on top of cake. Brush with lemon juice to prevent discoloration. Place a round of drained poached pineapple in center. Carefully brush top and sides of cake with warm Apricot Glaze. Fill the hole in the middle of the pineapple ring with a crown of chocolate pineapple leaves. Let cake rest in refrigerator for 1 hour to let thaw completely. Allow to stand at room temperature for 10 minutes before serving.

Use extra poached pineapple for another purpose—for example, a fruit compote. *Serves 8.*

· · · ◊ · · ·

OPÉRA CAKE

. . .

This is a classic chocolate-coffee cake that I believe was first made in the 1930s for an important French-American reception held at the Paris Opéra. I am sure that it contributed a great deal toward cordial relations! Layers of almond sponge are filled with a double filling of rich Kahlúa-flavored buttercream and chocolate-coffee ganache, and the cake is finished with a smooth chocolate glaze. Prepare espresso or cappuccino to serve with this cake: it is one of life's indulgences and simply out of this world.

Cake:

Traditional Almond Sponge sheet cake (recipe, page 130)

Kahlúa Syrup:

5 ounces (⅝ cup) Simple Syrup (recipe, page 237), combined with

5 ounces (⅝ cup) Kahlúa

Kahlúa Buttercream:

½ ounce (¼ cup) instant espresso powder

2 tablespoons boiling water

2 tablespoons Kahlúa

1 pint (2 cups) milk

4 egg yolks, large

4 ounces (½ cup) sugar

8 ounces (2 sticks) unsalted butter, soft

Mocha Ganache:

1 ounce (½ cup) instant espresso powder

2 tablespoons boiling water

1¼ pounds bittersweet chocolate

9 ounces (1⅛ cups) milk

2 ounces (¼ cup) Praliné Paste (recipe, page 248)

Chocolate Glaze:

4 ounces bittersweet chocolate
2 ounces (¼ cup) corn oil

Decoration:

3 Marzipan Acorns and 6 Marzipan Leaves (recipe, pages 247 and 246)

Make cake according to the recipe and let cool.

TO PREPARE BUTTERCREAM: Dissolve the instant espresso in boiling water and let cool. Stir in Kahlúa. Place milk in a saucepan and bring to a boil. In the meantime, beat egg yolks and sugar until light and lemon-colored. Whisk in a little of the boiling milk and then return entire mixture to saucepan. Do not allow it to boil again or the egg yolks will become grainy. Whisk constantly over moderate heat until mixture thickens and reaches 165° F. Custard should coat a spoon lightly. Transfer to a bowl and stir until cool. Cut butter into small cubes and beat into custard a little at a time at slow speed; then beat at high speed for 1 minute. Beat in espresso-Kahlúa flavoring. Refrigerate while preparing ganache.

TO MAKE MOCHA GANACHE: Dissolve the espresso in boiling water. Cut chocolate into small pieces and place in a bowl. Bring milk to a boil and pour over chocolate, stirring until completely smooth. Add the Praliné Paste and the espresso, and stir until mixture is smooth and shiny.

TO ASSEMBLE CAKE: Cut cake into four 5½-by-11-inch rectangles. Reserve the fourth layer for another use. Place one layer on a cake board and saturate cake with Kahlúa syrup. Spread with half the buttercream and then half the ganache. Top with a second layer of cake. Saturate with Kahlúa syrup and spread with layers of buttercream and ganache as before. Cover with third layer of cake and moisten well with Kahlúa syrup. Place in refrigerator for 4 hours.

***TO MAKE CHOCOLATE GLAZE*:** Cut chocolate into small pieces, place in a bowl, and melt over hot water. Stir in corn oil.

***TO DECORATE*:** Remove cake from refrigerator and pour the liquid chocolate glaze over top, tilting cake to help the glaze run. If using a long flexible baker's spatula to spread the glaze, do so quickly, as the glaze will set up fast on the cold cake. Refrigerate for 30 minutes to set completely. Remove cake from refrigerator and trim sides with a hot knife. (Dip blade of serrated bread knife in boiling water and dry before using.) Group marzipan acorns and leaves on top of cake. Allow to stand at room temperature for 15 minutes before serving.

Opéra Cake will keep for four to five days in the refrigerator. *Serves 8.*

· · · ◇ · · ·

CHARLENOIT CAKE

. . .

ADVANCED

In this cake, layers of hazelnut-almond meringue are sandwiched together with alternating fillings of silky chocolate cream and a rich Confectioners' Custard flavored with Praliné Paste. The contrast of flavors and textures is excellent.

Cake:

Hazelnut-Almond Meringue Sponge sheet cake (recipe, page 131)

Rum Syrup:

3 ounces (6 tablespoons) Simple Syrup (recipe, page 237), combined with
3 ounces (6 tablespoons) dark rum

Chocolate Cream:

8 ounces (1 cup) heavy cream
4 ounces (½ cup) sugar
4 ounces (1 cup) unsweetened cocoa powder
10 ounces unsalted butter, soft

Praliné Custard Cream:

10 ounces (1¼ cups) Confectioners' Custard (recipe, page 95)
1 ounce (¼ stick) unsalted butter, soft
10 ounces (1¼ cups) heavy cream
1 ounce (2 tablespoons) Praliné Paste (recipe, page 248)

Decoration:

4 ounces tinted pale green marzipan (page 243)
3 large hazelnuts

Prepare cake according to the recipe and let cool.

TO PREPARE THE CHOCOLATE CREAM: Combine cream with sugar in a small saucepan and bring to a boil. Sieve cocoa onto a sheet of paper and pour into cream. Whisk until smooth. Transfer mixture to bowl of electric mixer, let cool, and then refrigerate for 30 minutes. Remove from refrigerator and beat butter into cocoa-cream mixture a little at a time at low speed. Continue beating at high speed until mixture is smooth and shiny.

TO PREPARE THE PRALINÉ CUSTARD CREAM: Make Confectioners' Custard according to the recipe. It should be very thick. Pour into a bowl and, while it is still slightly warm, stir in the soft butter. Refrigerate until well chilled. Whip cream until soft peaks form and refrigerate. Remove custard from refrigerator and beat in Praliné Paste until mixture is smooth and light. Fold in whipped cream and refrigerate for at least 30 minutes.

TO ASSEMBLE CAKE: Cut sponge into 3 equal rectangles, approximately 5½-by-10 inches. Place one layer of cake on a cake board and saturate with rum syrup. Spread with half the chocolate cream. Top with second layer of cake and soak with syrup. Spread evenly with the praliné custard cream; it should be about 1 inch thick. Top with remaining layer of cake and soak with syrup. Place cake in freezer for 30 minutes. (If at any stage the fillings become too soft to hold their shape and keep the cake layers even, cover the cake closely with plastic and place in the freezer for a few minutes until it firms up.)

TO DECORATE: Remove cake from freezer and trim sides with a hot serrated bread knife (dip blade in boiling water and then dry). Transfer remaining chocolate cream to a pastry bag fitted with a narrow slit tip and cover top of cake with rows of tight S-shaped spirals.

....

Alternately, spread cake with remaining chocolate cream and make tight S-shaped lines with a decorating comb (see page 8). Place cake in refrigerator.

Roll out pale green marzipan ⅛ inch thick. Do this on a marble slab or between two sheets of plastic wrap. Cut out 3 circles of marzipan with a 1-inch scalloped cutter and wrap each one around a large hazelnut, like petals around the center of a flower. Cut out 6 marzipan leaves about 2½ inches long with a scalloped cutter and elongate them slightly with a rolling pin. Pinch closed at one end, like a real leaf. Group the leaves and the "fresh hazelnuts" on top of the cake. Refrigerate until 10 minutes before serving time.

The Charlenoit Cake will keep for three to four days in the refrigerator. *Serves 8.*

· · · ◊ · · ·

LIPPIZANER CAKE

. . .

This opulent cake is made by sandwiching two rectangles of Rich Chocolate-Almond Sponge together with a filling of extra-light, cherry-studded chocolate mousse. The top of the cake is covered with overlapping Chocolate Ruffles.

Cake:

Rich Chocolate Sponge sheet cake (recipe, page 132)

Kirsch Syrup:

5 ounces (⅝ cup) Simple Syrup (recipe, page 237), combined with
5 ounces (⅝ cup) Kirsch

Chocolate Parfait:

8 ounces bittersweet chocolate
½ ounces (2 envelopes) unflavored gelatin
1 tablespoon cold water
4 egg yolks, large
4 ounces (½ cup) Simple Syrup
4 egg whites, large
1 pint (2 cups) heavy cream

Cherry Filling:

13-ounce can pitted dark cherries in light syrup, drained

Decoration:

Chocolate Ruffles (recipe, page 242)
confectioners' sugar
unsweetened cocoa powder (optional)

Make cake according to the recipe and let cool.

TO MAKE THE CHOCOLATE PARFAIT: Cut up chocolate, place in a bowl, and melt over hot water. Set aside to cool so that it does not deflate your egg whites. Soften gelatin in cold water. Combine egg yolks and Simple Syrup in a large bowl. Set bowl over pan of simmering water; water must not touch bottom of bowl. Beat with a whisk or portable electric mixer until mixture doubles in volume and thickens, about 8 minutes. Remove from heat and stir in gelatin. Return to heat and whisk for a few seconds. In a separate bowl, beat egg whites to soft peaks. Pour cool but still liquid chocolate around edge of bowl containing egg yolk mixture, and lightly fold in. Pour egg-chocolate mixture over egg whites and fold together.

TO ASSEMBLE CAKE: Cut the chocolate sponge into two equal rectangles, approximately 10 by 7 inches each. Place one layer on a cake board or rectangle of cardboard covered with tin foil. Using a large pastry brush, saturate cake with Kirsch syrup. Cover with half the chocolate parfait. Stud the parfait with cherries, placing several around the edge so that they will show when the cake is trimmed. Spread with remaining parfait, reserving ½ cup for top of cake. Top with second layer of cake and saturate with Kirsch syrup. Place cake in freezer for 3 to 4 hours.

TO DECORATE: Make Chocolate Ruffles according to the recipe.
Remove cake from freezer and spread top with reserved chocolate parfait. Using a hot serrated bread knife (dip blade in boiling water and then dry), trim sides of cake evenly, slicing through cherries at edge of filling. Cover top of cake with Chocolate Ruffles, starting at one corner and fanning them out in diagonal rows. Refrigerate cake for 2 hours so that it can thaw. Sift confectioners' sugar lightly over the Chocolate Ruffles, and let cake stand at room temperature for 15 minutes before serving.

For a simpler presentation, remove cake from freezer and trim sides. Lay a sheet of paper diagonally across cake. Sift confectioners' sugar liberally over exposed surface. Remove paper and sift unsweetened cocoa powder over the other half of the cake. (To make a clean line between the cocoa and the confectioners' sugar, hold a wide-bladed knife at an angle across the cake, resting it lightly on the surface, as you apply the cocoa powder.)

The Lippizaner Cake will keep for four to five days in the refrigerator. *Serves 8.*

. . . ◊ . . .

GRAND MARNIER SOUFFLÉ CAKE

. . .

ADVANCED

In this dessert, a delicate Grand Marnier soufflé mixture is combined with chocolate sponge cake. You will need a cake ring or the rim from a springform pan to support the soufflé as it sets up. The soufflé, which is on top of as well as between the layers of cake, is finished with a brittle layer of glazed sugar. It is a very seductive combination!

Cake:

Rich Chocolate Sponge sheet cake (recipe, page 132)

Grand Marnier Syrup:

5 ounces (⅝ cup) Simple Syrup (recipe, page 237), combined with
5 ounces (⅝ cup) Grand Marnier

Grand Marnier Soufflé:

8 ounces (1 cup) milk
½ ounce (2 envelopes) unflavored gelatin
2 tablespoons cold water
3 egg yolks, large
5 ounces (⅔ cup) scant sugar
4 ounces (½ cup) Grand Marnier
3 egg whites, large
1 pint (2 cups) heavy cream

Decoration:

confectioners' sugar

TO PREPARE THE GRAND MARNIER SOUFFLÉ: Place milk in a saucepan and bring to a boil. Soak gelatin in cold water for 5 minutes. In the meantime, beat egg yolks with 2 ounces of the sugar until light and thick. Whisk a little of the boiling milk into the egg-sugar mixture and then return entire mixture to saucepan. Do not let it boil again or the egg yolks will become grainy. Whisk constantly over moderate heat, until the mixture thickens and reaches 165° F. on a candy thermometer. Custard should coat a spoon lightly. Pour a little of the hot custard over the gelatin, return this mixture to saucepan, and whisk for a few seconds. Transfer custard to a bowl and, stirring occasionally, let cool to room temperature. Do not allow mixture to set. Stir in Grand Marnier. In a large bowl, beat egg whites to soft peaks and slowly add remaining 3 ounces sugar. Keep beating until stiff peaks form. Add a little beaten egg white to the cooled custard to loosen the mixture, then fold the custard into the remaining egg whites. In a separate bowl, whip cream until it stands in soft peaks and fold into custard mixture.

TO ASSEMBLE DESSERT: Place the chocolate sheet cake on work surface and cut a strip off one side measuring 2 inches wide by 17 inches long. Cut out two 8-inch circles from remaining cake. Set a 9-inch-diameter by 3-inch-high cake ring on a cake board. Line sides of ring with the strip of cake, trimming to fit. Place one cake circle on bottom surface. Using a large pastry brush, saturate with Grand Marnier syrup. Fill cake shell with soufflé mixture until level with top of shell. Cover with second cake circle and saturate with Grand Marnier syrup. Carefully fill your mold (covering cake) with the remaining soufflé mixture until level with top of mold. Place in freezer for 3 to 4 hours.

Heat salamander* to almost red hot on top of stove. Remove cake from freezer and run a sharp knife around sides of ring. Place cake on a plate and sift confectioners' sugar liberally over top. Pass the salamander over the surface, almost but not quite touching it, and the sugar will caramelize into a thin, brittle sheet of golden sugar. Let cake thaw in refrigerator for 2 hours, and allow to stand at room temperature for 15 minutes before serving.

The Grand Marnier Soufflé Cake can be held in the refrigerator for up to one day before the sugar topping softens. *Serves 8.*

*A salamander, or Crème Brulée iron, is a small iron disk on a long handle. If you don't have one, you can caramelize the sugar topping by placing the dessert *very briefly* under a preheated broiler.

WASHINGTON CAKE

ADVANCED

I created this cake for American chocolate lovers: it has lots of character, like President George Washington! Three rectangular layers of Cointreau-moistened chocolate-almond sponge are filled with bittersweet chocolate mousse, and the cake is topped with chocolate curls.

Cake:

Rich Chocolate-Almond Sponge sheet cake (recipe, page 133)

Cointreau Syrup:

5 ounces (⅝ cup) Simple Syrup (recipe, page 237), combined with
5 ounces (⅝ cup) Cointreau

Bittersweet Chocolate Mousse:

4½ ounces bittersweet chocolate
2¾ ounces (¾ cup) scant unsweetened cocoa powder
1½ ounces (3 tablespoons) unsalted butter, soft
3 egg whites, large
2 ounces (¼ cup) generous sugar

Decoration:

bittersweet Chocolate Curls (recipe, page 242)
confectioners' sugar

Prepare sheet cake according to the recipe and let cool.

TO PREPARE THE BITTERSWEET CHOCOLATE MOUSSE: Cut up chocolate, place in a bowl, and melt over hot water. Remove from heat and let cool. Sift cocoa. Cut butter into cubes and melt until just creamy but do not allow to "break" and become oily, as this would cause the mousse to be less light. In a bowl combine butter and cocoa and mix until smooth. Beat the egg whites to soft peaks. Slowly add sugar and beat until stiff peaks form. Spoon the cocoa-butter mixture on top of the cool but still liquid chocolate. Stir in 2 tablespoons of the beaten egg white to loosen mixture. Pour the chocolate mixture over remaining egg whites and lightly fold together.

TO ASSEMBLE CAKE: Cut the chocolate sponge into 3 equal rectangles, about 10 by 5½ inches. Place one layer on a cake board or cardboard rectangle cut to size and covered with tin foil. Using a large pastry brush, soak cake with Cointreau syrup. Spread cake evenly with one-third of the chocolate mousse. Top with a second layer of cake, moisten with syrup, and spread with another layer of mousse. Cover with third layer of cake, soak with syrup, and spread with remaining chocolate mousse, saving 3 tablespoons for holding decoration on top of cake. Place cake in freezer for 1 hour.

TO DECORATE: Remove cake from freezer and spread with reserved chocolate mousse. Using a hot serrated bread knife (dip blade in very hot water and then dry), trim sides of cake evenly. Cover top of cake generously with Chocolate Curls. Lay a sheet of paper over one half of the cake, forming two triangles. Sift confectioners' sugar over the Chocolate Curls on the exposed half. Remove paper and refrigerate cake until required. Let cake stand at room temperature for 15 minutes before serving.

The Washington Cake will keep for up to four days in the refrigerator. *Serves 8.*

· · · ◇ · · ·

A R L E Q U I N   C A K E
. . .

A D V A N C E D

This three-layer chocolate-almond sponge cake is flavored with Scotch and has a "black-and-white" filling and decoration of alternating lines of dark chocolate and white chocolate mousse.

Cake:

Rich Chocolate-Almond Sponge sheet cake (recipe, page 133)

Scotch Syrup:

5 ounces (⅝ cup) Simple Syrup (recipe, page 237), combined with
5 ounces (⅝ cup) Scotch whisky

Bittersweet Chocolate Mousse:

8 ounces (1 cup) heavy cream
8 ounces bittersweet chocolate
4 ounces (1 stick) unsalted butter, soft

White Chocolate Mousse:

8 ounces (1 cup) heavy cream
8 ounces white chocolate
4 ounces (1 stick) unsalted butter, soft

TO MAKE THE CHOCOLATE MOUSSES: Both mousses are made the same way. Whip cream to soft peaks. Cut up dark chocolate and melt over low heat. Cut butter into cubes and stir in until mixture is smooth. Let cool. Fold cream into cooled but still liquid chocolate-butter mixture. Follow same procedure with ingredients for white chocolate mousse.

. . . .

TO ASSEMBLE CAKE: Cut the chocolate-almond sponge into four rectangles, 5½ by 8½ inches and save the fourth layer for another use. Place one layer on a cake board and saturate with Scotch syrup. Transfer light and dark chocolate mousses to two pastry bags fitted with plain round ½-inch tips. Pipe alternating lines of dark and white chocolate mousse across the short side of the cake. The stripes must touch each other. Cover with second layer of cake and soak with syrup as before. Press down very gently. Pipe with lines of dark and white chocolate mousse, reversing the order used on the first layer. Top with third layer of cake and saturate with syrup. Again press down very gently, to make level. Starting at one corner, pipe diagonal stripes of light and dark chocolate mousse on top of cake. Freeze cake for 30 minutes.

Using a hot serrated bread knife (dip blade in boiling water, then dry), trim sides of cake. Refrigerate cake until required. Let stand at room temperature for 10 minutes before serving.

The Arlequin Cake will keep for two or three days in the refrigerator. *Serves 8*.

. . . ◊ . . .

JESTER CAKE

. . .

Rich but not too sweet, this elegant cake is formed from sheets of coffee and chocolate génoise. The sheets of sponge are cut into small triangles for the sides and into large circles for the bottom, middle, and top. (You will need a cake ring [page 6] or the rim of a springform pan to assemble it.) The cake is sandwiched together with chocolate ganache and chopped toasted hazelnuts and finished with a smooth chocolate glaze.

Cakes:

Rich Chocolate-Almond Sponge (recipe, page 133) and Coffee Génoise (recipe, page 134)

Kahlúa Rum Syrup:

4 ounces (½ cup) Simple Syrup (recipe, page 237), combined with
2 tablespoons Kahlúa
and
2 tablespoons dark rum

Hazelnut Decoration and Filling:

4 ounces (⅔ cup) hazelnuts

Chocolate Ganache:

6 ounces (1½ sticks) unsalted butter, soft
2 ounces (½ cup) confectioners' sugar
1 pound bittersweet chocolate
8 ounces (1 cup) milk

Chocolate Glaze:

4 ounces bittersweet chocolate

2 ounces (¼ cup) corn oil

Make sheet cakes according to the recipes and let cool.

TO MAKE THE HAZELNUT DECORATION AND FILLING: Preheat oven to 350°F. Spread nuts out on a baking sheet and toast until lightly browned, 12 to 15 minutes. Pour onto a clean kitchen towel and rub nuts together with the towel to remove skins. Reserve 18 nuts for top of cake and coarsely chop the remainder.

TO MAKE THE CHOCOLATE GANACHE: Beat butter and confectioners' sugar together until light and creamy, and set aside. Cut chocolate into small pieces and place in a bowl. Bring milk to a boil and pour over chocolate, stirring until melted and smooth. Let cool. While still liquid, beat in the butter-sugar mixture.

TO ASSEMBLE CAKE: Cut a 2¾-by-17-inch strip from both the sheet cakes. Using a cake pan as a guide, cut an 8-inch circle from the remaining coffee-flavored cake and two 8-inch circles from the remaining chocolate cake. Stack the two strips of cake on top of each other, smooth sides together, and make diagonal cuts, forming 2¾-inch-high triangles. (By cutting the triangles simultaneously, they will fit together properly.) Place a 9-inch cake ring on a cake board and line the sides with triangles of cake, alternating the coffee and chocolate flavors and fitting them snugly together. Make sure that the smooth sides face inward. Lay one of the chocolate cake circles in the bottom of the ring and brush generously with Kahlúa-rum syrup. Spread with half the chocolate ganache and sprinkle with half the chopped hazelnuts. Lay the coffee-flavored circle of cake on top and brush well with syrup. Spread with remaining ganache, saving 2 teaspoons for securing nuts on top of cake. Sprinkle with rest of chopped hazelnuts and cover with remaining circle of Chocolate Génoise.

The assembled cake should be about ¼ inch below the top of the cake ring. Brush cake generously with remaining syrup. Arrange reserved whole hazelnuts on top in one outer circle and one inner circle, securing them with a dot of ganache. Freeze cake for 2 hours.

TO MAKE THE CHOCOLATE GLAZE: Cut chocolate into small pieces, place in a bowl, and melt over hot water. Stir in corn oil.

Remove cake from freezer and quickly pour liquid glaze over the top, covering the hazelnuts, and tilting the cake to let the glaze run. This step is almost sure to be a little messy! Wipe excess chocolate off cake ring and refrigerate cake for 30 minutes to set. Run a sharp knife inside ring and then lift it off the cake. Return cake to refrigerator to thaw completely, about 1 hour. Transfer cake to serving plate and allow cake to stand at room temperature for 15 minutes before serving. Cut with a hot knife.

The Jester Cake will keep for four to five days in the refrigerator. *Serves 8.*

· · · ◇ · · ·

CHOCOLATE CHARLOTTE

. . .

ADVANCED

This dessert is made by lining a cake ring with a band of soft sponge ladyfingers. The bottom is covered with a layer of sponge cake, and the cake is filled with smooth chocolate mousse. The top is covered with dark chocolate curls, and I tie a wide red ribbon around the cake. I recommend making both the ladyfingers and the génoise the day before the charlotte is to be assembled.

Cake:

Ladyfingers (recipe, page 135) and Traditional Génoise Sponge
    (recipe, page 125)

Chocolate Mousse:

9 ounces bittersweet chocolate
4 ounces (1 stick) unsalted butter, soft, cut in cubes
3 egg yolks, large
3 tablespoons Simple Syrup (recipe, page 237)
1 tablespoon dark rum
8 egg whites, large
2 ounces (¼ cup) generous sugar

Rum Syrup:

4 ounces (½ cup) Simple Syrup (recipe, page 237)
4 ounces (½ cup) dark rum

Decoration:

dark Chocolate Curls (recipe, page 242)

....

Make ladyfingers according to the recipe. Pipe the fingers onto a parchment-lined baking sheet, making them 2½ inches high and forming a 14-inch-long band. The ladyfingers should touch each other. (Pipe out single ladyfingers with remaining batter and reserve for another use.) Dust with confectioners' sugar and bake at 400°F. for 8 minutes and let cool on rack. Make Traditional Génoise according to recipe.

TO MAKE MOUSSE: Cut up chocolate, place in a large bowl, and melt over hot water. Stir in butter and let cool. Place egg yolks and Simple Syrup in a large metal bowl and whisk over simmering water until very pale in color and thickened. Add rum. Whip egg whites until soft peaks start to form. Slowly add sugar, then beat mixture until stiff and glossy. Pour the egg-yolk mixture into the cooled but still liquid chocolate with one-third of the egg whites. Mix together, then fold gently into remaining egg whites.

TO ASSEMBLE CAKE: Place a 9-inch cake ring (or the rim from a springform pan) on a cake board or flat plate. Cut the rounded ends off one side of the band of ladyfingers and set the band inside the cake ring, straight side down, and curved side facing outward. Cut to fit exactly. Slice génoise in half horizontally, and trim to fit inside border of ladyfingers. Place one of the layers inside the ring. Saturate with rum syrup and add half the chocolate mousse. Cover with remaining layer of génoise, soaking it well with rum syrup. Top with remaining chocolate mousse and refrigerate cake for 1 hour.

Remove cake ring and cover top of charlotte generously with chocolate curls. Tie ribbon around sides. Refrigerate charlotte until serving time.

A Chocolate Charlotte will keep for one day in the refrigerator. *Serves 8.*

10.

Cookies

· · · ◇ · · ·

Always popular, cookies are simple to make and have the added virtue of keeping well if stored airtight. (Do not mix different types in the same container; the crisper types will inevitably soften.) For the best results, it is important to have all your cookies the same thickness and size, so that they bake evenly, and I recommend that you chill your short doughs before baking. Naturally you don't have to, but it firms up the butter and the cookies then hold their shape in the oven and have a better texture.

The recipes in this section are for various kinds of short dough or butter cookies, wafers, and macaroons. Additional excellent crisp cookies such as Palmiers and Bamboo will be found in the puff doughs section.

Index:

· · · ◇ · · ·

Cookies

PIPED BUTTER COOKIES

. . .

*These excellent cookies are sold by the kilo in France, regardless of shape
or size. They are extremely easy to make, and you can form them into any
shape you please: stars, shells, or S-shapes. I usually add a nutmeat, a
lozenge of candied peel, or some jam to each cookie before baking. If you
wish, you can dust them with confectioners' sugar when cool.*

8 ounces (1 cup) generous sugar
8 ounces (2 sticks) lightly salted butter, soft
2 eggs, large
1 teaspoon vanilla extract
1 teaspoon rum extract
11 ounces (2¼ cups) all-purpose flour

Preheat oven to 400°F. Line two baking sheets with baking parchment. Fit a pastry bag with a large open star tube.

In bowl of electric mixer, beat sugar and butter together until light
and fluffy. Add eggs, vanilla and rum extracts. Pour flour on top
and beat until smooth but do not overwork dough. Transfer to pastry
bag and pipe out 2-inch cookies (see illustration) on prepared baking
sheets. Decorate as desired. Refrigerate for 15 minutes so that butter
firms up and cookies do not lose their shape in the oven. Bake for
15 to 20 minutes until lightly colored. Cool on racks. *Makes approximately 75.*

RASPBERRY
WINDOW COOKIES

· · ·

These simple and satisfying cookies are made by sandwiching baked ovals or rounds of sugar dough together with raspberry jam. The top cookie is pierced with two holes, so that the filling shows through, and the cookies are dusted with confectioners' sugar.

8 ounces Pâte Sucrée (half quantity of recipe, page 25)
4 ounces (½ cup) raspberry jam
confectioners' sugar

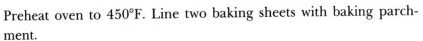

Preheat oven to 450°F. Line two baking sheets with baking parchment.

On a lightly floured surface, roll dough out ¼-inch thick. With a fluted 4-inch oval or round cutter, cut out as many cookies as possible. Using a ½-inch round cutter, make two holes in half the cookies (see illustration). Reroll and cut trimmings. Transfer cookies to prepared baking sheets. Refrigerate for 15 minutes.

Bake cookies for 12 to 15 minutes, until pale gold. Cool on racks. Spread the solid cookies with a thin layer of raspberry jam. Dust pierced cookies with confectioners' sugar and place on top of solid cookies. *Makes approximately 20.*

· · · ◊ · · ·

SABLÉS DE CAEN

(Orange Shortbreads)

. . .

EASY

These orange-flavored shortbread cookies have a very fine texture. Be careful not to overboil the eggs, or you might get a flavor of sulfur—9 minutes in gently boiling water is sufficient.

3 eggs, large, hard-boiled and cooled
10 ounces (2 cups) all-purpose flour
4 ounces (½ cup) sugar
zest of half an orange (colored part only), finely chopped
1 teaspoon orange flower water (page 3)
8 ounces (2 sticks) lightly salted butter, soft

Sieve the egg yolks and set aside, discarding the whites. In bowl of electric mixer, combine flour, sugar, orange rind, orange flower water, and sieved egg yolks. Beat until blended. Cut butter into cubes and add to bowl. Mix dough until smooth but do not overwork. Gather dough into a ball, enclose in plastic wrap, and refrigerate for 1 hour.

Preheat oven to 400°F. Line two baking sheets with baking parchment.

On a lightly floured surface, roll dough out ¼ inch thick. Cut with a fluted cutter into 4-inch rounds. Score lightly with a fork to make an allover grid pattern. Transfer rounds to prepared baking sheets and refrigerate for 15 minutes. Cut each round into 4 quarters and separate them from each other. Bake for 15 minutes, until pale gold. *Makes 36 triangular cookies.*

SABLÉS DE NANTES

(Coffee-flavored Cookies with Chocolate)

. . .

INTERMEDIATE

The best butter in France comes from Normandy, Brittany, and the area around Charentes, and each region—and sometimes each town—has its own traditional butter cookies. The crisp, coffee-flavored Sablés de Nantes, with the characteristic glazed crisscross pattern on top, can be left plain or coated on the smooth side with bittersweet chocolate.

6 ounces (¾ cup) scant sugar
2 teaspoons packed dark brown sugar
4 ounces (1 stick) lightly salted butter, soft
1 egg, large
1 egg yolk, large
½ teaspoon vanilla extract
1 teaspoon instant powdered espresso coffee
8 ounces (1½ cups) all-purpose flour
1 egg yolk, for glaze
1 tablespoon very strong coffee, preferably espresso, cold
4 ounces bittersweet chocolate, melted (optional)

In bowl of electric mixer, combine white and brown sugar. Cut the butter into cubes and add to mixture. Beat together until light and fluffy. Add the whole egg, the egg yolk, vanilla extract, and powdered coffee. Pour flour over mixture and beat only until smooth. Do not overwork the dough. Gather dough into a ball, cover with plastic wrap, and refrigerate for 30 minutes.

Preheat oven to 400°F. Line two large baking sheets with baking parchment. On a lightly floured board, roll dough out ⅛ inch thick. With a 2½-inch round fluted cutter, cut into rounds. Reroll and cut the trimmings. Transfer cookies to prepared baking sheets and refrigerate for 15 minutes.

Blend egg yolk with the cold coffee and brush over cookies. With a fork, mark a crisscross pattern on each one. Bake for 8 to 10 minutes, until lightly colored. Cool on rack. If desired, coat the smooth side of the cookies with chocolate and let set. *Makes approximately 24.*

· · · ◇ · · ·

GALETTE BRETONNE

(Shortcake with Candied Fruit)

· · ·

INTERMEDIATE

Rich, buttery, and scented with orange flower water, this specialty of Brittany is cut in wedges to serve. The dough is very soft, so the galette is baked in a pastry ring (see page 6).

8½ ounces (2 sticks plus 1 tablespoon) lightly salted butter, soft
6 ounces (¾ cup) sugar
1 egg, large
1 egg yolk, large
1 teaspoon orange flower water (page 3)
8½ ounces (1½ cups plus 2 tablespoons) all-purpose flour
1 teaspoon baking powder
6 ounces (1 cup) diced mixed candied peel
1 egg yolk, for glaze
2 teaspoons water

Butter a 9-by-1½-inch-high pastry ring. Line a baking sheet with baking parchment and place the ring on it.

Beat butter and sugar together until light and fluffy. Add the whole egg, the egg yolk, and orange flower water. Mix well. Add flour and baking powder. Beat until smooth, then stir in the candied peel.

Spread dough evenly inside pastry ring. Smooth the top and refrigerate for 1 hour.

Preheat oven to 350°F. Mix egg yolk with water and brush top of galette. Mark with a fork at 1½-inch intervals, crossing the first lines at an angle to form large diamonds. Bake for 30 minutes or until a deep gold. Let cool for 5 minutes before removing ring. Transfer galette to rack (the base from a loose-bottomed quiche pan makes a convenient outside "spatula") and let cool. *Serves 8.*

·   ·   ·   ◇   ·   ·   ·

S U L T A N S

(Raisin-Rum Cookies)

·   ·   ·

E A S Y

2½ ounces (½ cup) yellow raisins
2 tablespoons dark rum
8 ounces (2 sticks) lightly salted butter, soft
8 ounces (1 cup) generous sugar
4 egg yolks, large
½ teaspoon rum extract
½ teaspoon vanilla extract
10 ounces (2 cups) all-purpose flour

Soak raisins in dark rum for 30 minutes.

Preheat oven to 400°F. Line two large baking sheets with baking parchment. Fit a pastry bag with a plain round ½-inch tube.

In bowl of electric mixer, combine butter and sugar. Beat until light and fluffy. Add the egg yolks, rum extract, and vanilla and stir well. Beat in the flour but do not overmix dough at this point or cookies will be heavy. Stir in drained raisins. Transfer mixture to pastry bag and pipe out 1-inch mounds. Chill for 15 minutes.

Bake cookies for 10 minutes, until lightly colored, and cool on rack. *Makes approximately 60.*

. . . ◊ . . .

ORANGE-CHOCOLATE TRIANGLES
. . .

INTERMEDIATE

6 ounces (¾ cup) scant sugar
2 eggs, large
1 egg yolk, large
4½ ounces (1⅛ sticks) unsalted butter, soft
12 ounces (2½ cups) scant all-purpose flour
1 ounce (2 tablespoons) Candied Orange Peel (recipe, page 214), or use store-bought variety
½ teaspoon baking powder
1 egg yolk, for glaze
2 teaspoons cold water
4 ounces bittersweet chocolate, melted

In bowl of electric mixer, combine sugar, whole eggs, and egg yolk. Cut butter into cubes and beat into sugar-egg mixture. Put a little of the flour on work surface and add orange peel. Cut into tiny slivers—the flour will prevent peel from sticking to the knife. Add remaining flour, baking powder, and slivered orange peel to bowl and mix quickly. The dough will be very soft. Gather into a ball, enclose in plastic, and chill for 30 minutes.

Line two baking sheets with baking parchment. On a lightly floured surface, roll dough out ¼ inch thick. Cut the sheet of dough into 3-inch wide strips and then into triangles. Transfer triangles to baking sheets and refrigerate for 15 minutes.

Preheat oven to 425°F. Blend egg yolk with cold water and brush over cookies. Bake for 10 to 12 minutes, until lightly colored. Let cool on racks. Holding each cookie at the center between thumb and forefinger, dip all three edges in warm chocolate. Lay on baking parchment or tin foil until set. *Makes approximately 30.*

$$\cdots \ \Diamond \ \cdots$$

F L O R E N T I N E   C O O K I E S

(Sugar Dough with Almond/Candied Peel/Honey)

· · ·

A D V A N C E D

Dough:

1 pound Pâte Sucrée (recipe, page 25)

Topping:

¾ ounce (3 tablespoons) all-purpose flour
4 ounces (½ cup) Candied Orange Peel (recipe, page 214), or
use store-bought variety
3 ounces (½ cup) candied cherries*
7 ounces (1½ cups) slivered almonds
5 ounces (⅔ cup) scant sugar
2½ ounces (5 tablespoons) lightly salted butter

*Rinse commercial candied cherries in boiling water to remove excess red syrup; drain and pat dry on paper towels.

2 ounces (4 tablespoons) honey
2½ ounces (5 tablespoons) heavy cream
4 ounces bittersweet chocolate, melted

Preheat oven to 425°F. Line a baking sheet with baking parchment. On a lightly floured surface, roll Pâte Sucrée ⅛ inch thick and trim to a 15-by-9-inch rectangle. Refrigerate while preparing topping.

On a board, combine flour, orange peel, and cherries. Chop fine, add almonds, and set aside. In a heavy saucepan combine sugar, butter, honey, and cream. Bring to a boil and let cook for 3 to 4 minutes, stirring. Mixture should brown slightly and pull away from sides of pan. Add fruit mixture, stir well, and remove from heat. Spread topping evenly over chilled dough. Bake for 20 minutes. While still warm, cut into 1½-inch squares, separate, and let cool on racks. Dip one corner of each Florentine in the melted chocolate and place on aluminum foil to set. *Makes approximately 60.*

· · · ◊ · · ·

T U I L E S

(Almond Wafers)

. . .

INTERMEDIATE

These crispy wafers get their name from old-fashioned curved clay roofing tiles. As soon as they come out of the oven they must be molded into shape, while still hot and pliable. I place them inside a shallow savarin mold or bend them over a large rolling pin. When the Tuiles have cooled completely, store them in an airtight container so they will not lose their crispness.

2½ ounces (½ cup) sliced almonds, finely chopped
2½ ounces (½ cup) generous confectioners' sugar
1¼ ounces (¼ cup) all-purpose flour
1 egg yolk, large
2 egg whites, large
¼ teaspoon vanilla extract

Preheat oven to 475°F. Grease two large baking sheets with butter.

Combine chopped almonds, confectioners' sugar, and flour. Beat the egg yolk and egg whites with vanilla to a smooth emulsion. Mix with dry ingredients and let batter rest for 10 minutes to thicken slightly.

Make only 4 to 6 Tuiles at a time, so they do not firm up too quickly to mold. Drop batter by tablespoonsful, 3 inches apart, on prepared baking sheet. Bang it sharply on countertop to make the batter spread out or spread with the back of a spoon to 4-inch circles. Bake for 5 minutes, until wafers start to color at edges. Remove from baking sheet immediately with a pastry scraper and bend into shape while still hot and pliable. (The cookies will firm up almost immediately, and can then be transferred to a rack.) Repeat until all the batter is used, using the two baking sheets alternately. *Makes approximately 30.*

CIGARETTES

(Rolled Wafers)

. . .

ADVANCED

These melt-in-the-mouth rolled wafers take only 5 minutes to bake. Roll them around the handle of a wooden spoon as soon as they come out of the oven so they do not become too brittle to roll. Do not bake more than six at a time.

6 ounces (¾ cup) scant sugar
4 egg whites, large
½ teaspoon vanilla extract
4 ounces (1 stick) unsalted butter, melted and cooled to lukewarm
2½ ounces (½ cup) all-purpose flour

Preheat oven to 450°F. Butter two large baking sheets generously.

Combine sugar and egg whites and beat until very smooth. Stir in vanilla and butter. Add flour and mix until just blended. Let batter stand for 10 minutes to thicken slightly. Drop by teaspoonful onto prepared baking sheet at widely spaced intervals. Bang the baking sheet sharply on countertop to spread batter or spread out with the back of a spoon to 4-inch circles. Bake for 5 minutes, until wafers are pale gold and beginning to brown at the edges. Immediately remove the first wafer from baking sheet with a pastry scraper and roll tightly around the handle of a wooden spoon. Press down lightly to seal. Remove and roll remaining wafers. Repeat procedure with rest of batter. *Makes approximately 30.*

. . . ◇ . . .

ZEBRAS

(Rolled Wafers with Coffee Stripes)

· · ·

Proceed as above for Cigarettes, reserving a quarter cup of batter. Stir in ½ teaspoon coffee extract. Transfer mixture to a small cone made of baking parchment (see page 5 for directions) and pipe four thin lines across each circle of batter. Draw the back of a knife blade across the lines at right angles to make a feather design. Bake and then roll as above, striped side out.

· · · ◊ · · ·

BÂTONS DE MARÉCHAL

(Almond Macaroon Fingers with Chocolate)

· · ·

INTERMEDIATE

These delicious finger-sized macaroon cookies have chopped almonds on top and a thin layer of chocolate on the underside. They should be slightly chewy, not crisp.

4½ ounces (1 cup plus 2 tablespoons) almond meal (page 1)
4 ounces (½ cup) sugar
1 egg yolk, large
2 egg whites, large
3 tablespoons slivered almonds, chopped
4 ounces bittersweet chocolate, melted

Preheat oven to 425°F. Line a baking sheet with baking parchment. Fit a pastry bag with a ¼-inch plain round tip.

Combine almond meal and sugar and blend in egg yolk. Mixture will be dry and crumbly. Whip egg whites until stiff. Fold the almond-sugar mixture gently into the egg whites, deflating the mixture as little as possible. Transfer to pastry bag and pipe out 2½-inch fingers on prepared baking sheet. Sprinkle with chopped almonds. Bake for 8 to 10 minutes until just starting to color. Let cool on rack.

Spread the flat underside of each cookie with a thin layer of melted chocolate and leave upside down on rack until glaze hardens. *Makes approximately 36.*

· · · ◇ · · ·

A L M O N D   M A C A R O O N S
· · ·

E A S Y

Unlike Italian amaretti, which are made from similar ingredients but which are baked until dry and crisp, these macaroons are meant to be crisp on the outside and chewy within. You will obtain the finest results using a food processor, but very good macaroons can be made using a mixer or blending by hand.

9 ounces almond paste (page 1)
5 ounces (⅔ cup) scant sugar
2 teaspoons smooth apricot jam
2 egg whites, large

Preheat oven to 375°F. Line a baking sheet with baking parchment. Fit a pastry bag with a ½-inch plain round tip.

In bowl of food processor, combine almond paste, sugar, apricot jam, and egg whites. Process until smooth. Transfer to pastry bag and pipe out 1-inch mounds on prepared baking sheets.

Bake macaroons for 12 to 15 minutes until lightly colored and crisp. Allow to cool on the parchment paper. Turn the paper over,

· ·

macaroons and all, and moisten the reverse with a damp cloth. In a few minutes the macaroons will come away from the baking parchment easily.

If you wish to stick the macaroons together in pairs, pour a little water under the parchment paper as soon as the baking sheet is removed from the oven. The resultant steam will release the macaroons from the paper. Immediately match back to back in pairs and they will stick together. *Makes approximately 40.*

. . . ◊ . . .

PASTEL MACAROONS
. . .

INTERMEDIATE

These extra-delicate, fine-textured macaroons are made in just the same way as plain Almond Macaroons (recipe, page 189), but must be allowed to rest for 3 hours before baking.

9 ounces almond paste (page 1)
7 egg whites, large
1 teaspoon raspberry extract
2 drops red food coloring
14 ounces (1¾ cups) sugar

Line two large baking sheets with baking parchment. Fit pastry bag with a plain round ½-inch tip.

Beat or knead almond paste with 1 egg white, raspberry extract, and red food coloring. Set aside. In bowl of electric mixer, whip egg whites until soft peaks form, then add sugar. Beat at medium-high speed until very stiff and glossy. Blend in the almond paste. Transfer to pastry bag and pipe out 1-inch mounds on the prepared baking sheets. Let dry for 3 hours so that macaroons form a light crust. This prevents them from collapsing in the oven.

Preheat oven to 275°F. Bake macaroons for 25 minutes, until lightly colored and crisp. To release macaroons from baking parchment, see instructions for Almond Macaroons on page 189. *Makes approximately 100.*

COFFEE MACAROONS: Substitute 1 teaspoon coffee extract for the raspberry extract and omit food coloring.

LEMON MACAROONS: Substitute 1 teaspoon lemon extract for the raspberry extract and use 2 drops yellow food coloring instead of red.

. . . ◊ . . .

COCONUT MACAROONS
. . .

INTERMEDIATE

4 ounces (½ cup) sugar
1 egg white, large
4 ounces (⅔ cup) flaked unsweetened coconut
1 whole egg, large
½ teaspoon vanilla extract

Preheat oven to 350°F. Line a baking sheet with baking parchment and fit a pastry bag with a plain round ½-inch tube.

Place sugar and egg white in a saucepan and beat over low heat until the mixture is warm to the touch. Remove from heat and beat in coconut, whole egg, and vanilla. Transfer mixture to pastry bag and pipe out 1-inch mounds onto prepared baking sheet. Bake for 15 minutes, until lightly colored. Cool on rack. *Makes approximately 20.*

D U C H E S S E

(Hazelnut Macaroons)

. . .

I N T E R M E D I A T E

3 egg whites, large
4½ ounces (½ cup) generous sugar
4½ ounces (¼ cups) finely ground hazelnuts*
2 ounces (½ cup) scant all-purpose flour
4 tablespoons milk
2 ounces (½ stick) unsalted butter, melted
Apricot Glaze (recipe, page 241)

Preheat oven to 425°F. Line a baking sheet with baking parchment.
Fit a pastry bag with a plain round ½-inch tip.

Whisk egg whites until soft peaks form. Slowly add 2 ounces of
the sugar and continue whisking until stiff and glossy. In a separate
bowl combine remaining sugar with ground hazelnuts and flour. Add
milk and melted butter and stir well. Loosen mixture with a little of
the beaten egg white, then pile remaining egg white on top and fold
in. Transfer to pastry bag. Pipe 1-inch mounds onto prepared baking
sheet. Bake for 12 minutes, until lightly colored. Let cool on parchment paper. Turn paper over, cookies and all, and moisten back with
a damp cloth. Within a few minutes the cookies will come free easily.
Brush tops with warm Apricot Glaze. *Makes approximately 40.*

*If grinding hazelnuts in a food processor, add a little of the sugar to help
prevent nuts from becoming oily.

11

Meringue & Uses

· · · ◇ · · ·

Meringue is basically a mixture of stiffly beaten egg white and sugar and can be made by three different classic methods.

French Meringue, which is the most delicate and fragile, and therefore breaks more easily, is made with stiffly beaten egg white and uncooked sugar, half of which is beaten in and the other half folded in. It is the simplest to make and can be used for all the meringue preparations listed in this chapter.

Swiss Meringue is made by heating egg whites and sugar to 120°F. The mixture is then beaten until well aerated, stiff, and shiny. It is less fragile than French Meringue and keeps better. It is very useful for meringue shells and small decorations, such as meringue mushrooms.

Italian Meringue is made by pouring sugar cooked to the hard ball stage over beaten egg whites. The mixture is then beaten until stiff and glossy. This type of meringue is preferred for use in certain pastry creams.

Meringue mixtures with the addition of ground nuts, sometimes called japonais mixtures, require careful handling because the oil in the nuts can cause the meringue to collapse. The nuts have to be folded in quickly and lightly to ensure success.

It's best not to try to bake crisp meringues on a wet day: the humidity in the air will soften your meringue as it cools. I have trouble with meringue mixtures in foggy San Francisco!

Egg whites freeze successfully, as does baked meringue, and it is useful to remember that 1 large egg white weighs about $1^{1}/_{4}$ ounces, so 3 will equal about $^{1}/_{2}$ cup.

Index:

. . . ◊ . . .

Meringue & Uses

Basic Meringue

· · · ◇ · · ·

FRENCH MERINGUE

· · ·

EASY

4 egg whites, large
7 ounces (¾ cup) generous sugar
7 ounces (1¾ cups) confectioners' sugar

Preheat oven to 200°F. Line one or two baking sheets with baking parchment. If required, draw circles or ovals of the desired size on the underside of the baking parchment as guidelines.

Place egg whites in bowl of electric mixer and whip at medium speed until they start to hold their shape. Add the granulated sugar slowly, at low speed, then increase speed to medium high and whip until mixture is very stiff and shiny and holds a stiff, unwavering peak. Remove bowl from stand and fold in the confectioners' sugar.

Transfer mixture to a pastry bag fitted with a plain ½-inch tube and pipe out desired shapes: one large round or oval shell with 2-inch-high sides, six to eight individual shells, or meringue mushrooms and stalks. Bake for 1 to 2 hours—this is not so much baking as drying out. The meringues should not color and should be very dry and crisp. Let cool and store airtight if not for immediate use. Meringue will keep for two weeks.

· · · ◇ · · ·

SWISS MERINGUE

. . .

INTERMEDIATE

4 egg whites, large
12 ounces (1½ cups) sugar

Preheat oven to 200°F. Line two baking sheets with baking parchment.

Combine egg whites and sugar in bowl of electric mixer. Set bowl over a pan of simmering water. Beat mixture with a whisk or hand-held electric mixer until it thickens and reaches 120°F. Place bowl on mixer stand and whip at medium-high speed until mixture is cold, about 10 minutes. The meringue will increase greatly in volume and should be very stiff.

Transfer mixture to a pastry bag and pipe out desired shapes— one large shell for filling with fruit or cream; six individual shells; or meringue mushrooms. Bake for 1 to 2 hours to dry out completely. The meringues should not color. Let cool and store airtight if not for immediate use. Meringue will keep for two weeks.

. . . ◇ . . .

ITALIAN MERINGUE

· · ·

4 egg whites, large
8 ounces (1 cup) generous sugar
5 ounces (⅝ cup) water

Preheat oven to 200°F. Line two baking sheets with baking parchment.

Place egg whites in bowl of electric mixer and whip until stiff. Combine sugar and water in a heavy pan, preferably of unlined copper, and boil to the hard ball stage, 250°F. Remove bowl from stand and pour sugar syrup slowly into beaten egg whites, beating constantly with a hand whisk (the machine tends to spatter too much during this operation). Return bowl to stand and whip at medium speed until meringue is cold, well aerated, and very stiff.

Transfer mixture to a pastry bag and pipe out desired shapes— one large shell for filling with fruit or cream and eight individual shells; or make meringue mushrooms. Bake for 1 to 2 hours to dry out completely. The meringues should not color. Let cool and store airtight. Meringue will keep for two weeks.

· · · ◇ · · ·

· ·

Techniques

· · · ◊ · · ·

LARGE AND INDIVIDUAL MERINGUE SHELLS

When baked and cooled, meringue shells can be filled with fresh fruit, berries, whipped cream or custard, or ice cream.

Line a baking sheet with baking parchment. If you require a guideline, draw an 8-to-9-inch circle or oval of the required size on the underside of the paper, so that pencil graphite does not get onto your meringue. Fill a pastry bag fitted with a plain ½-inch tube with meringue mixture of choice. Starting at the inside rim of the circle, pipe a ½-inch-diameter line of meringue, decreasing the size of the spiral until you reach the center. Make sure the edges of the spirals touch each other. To form the sides, pipe a circle of meringue on top of this base, around the edge. Pipe a second circle inside and touching the first one. Pipe a third circle on top of the first two, pyramid fashion.

To make individual meringue shells, use a ¼-inch tip and pipe spirals from 3 to 4 inches in diameter. Form the sides by piping two circles on top of each other around the rim.

· · · ◊ · · ·

MERINGUE MUSHROOMS

. . .

Form the caps by piping neat mushroom-size mounds onto a baking sheet lined with baking parchment. Slice off any "peaks" with a knife. Dust lightly with cocoa powder, shaking it through a sieve, to imitate a little earth or humus. Pipe an equal number of slender pointed "stalks." Bake at 200°F. for about 1 hour, until dry and crisp. Let cool. Using the tip of a small knife, hollow out the center of each "mushroom cap." Dip the pointed end of each stalk in melted and cooled semisweet chocolate and insert into the cap. Allow to harden. The chocolate will hold the stalk in place and resemble the brown gills of a field mushroom. Use meringue mushrooms to decorate a Bûche de Noël (recipe, page 210), or pack into small baskets for presentation as candy.

MERINGUE SHOES

. . .

In Europe, Saint Nicholas leaves children's gifts in boots, not stockings. According to legend, his magical sleigh is drawn through the air by a horse. This equippage comes to rest on rooftops, and Saint Nicholas sends his servant, Black Peter, down the chimney. Children leave their boots by the fireside filled with gifts of hay and carrots for the horse, which Black Peter takes and replaces with gifts. One consequence of this delightful story is that a little pair of meringue boots often decorates a Bûche de Noël. To make them, pipe out the "feet" first. Then hold a smaller tip over the larger tip and pipe out a little hollow spiral on the narrower end of each foot to form the ankle of the boot. If you like, position three small silver dragées* down the front of each boot to imitate buttons.

*Dragées are small edible decorations of silvered sugar, in the shape of tiny balls. They are available in the spice or cake ingredient department of most supermarkets.

....

Gâteaux

. . . ◇ . . .

N O I S E T T E

(Meringue Layer Cake with Hazelnut Buttercream)

. . .

A D V A N C E D

My version of this classic nineteenth-century French cake is lighter and less sweet than the original. It is an irresistible combination of crisp nut meringue with a smooth buttercream filling, and is served with a hazelnut-coffee sauce.

Nut Meringue Layers:

4 egg whites, large
5 ounces (²/₃ cup) scant sugar
2½ ounces (½ cup) generous confectioners' sugar
2½ ounces (½ cup plus 2 tablespoons) almond meal (page 1)
1 tablespoon milk

Hazelnut Buttercream:

4 ounces (½ cup) milk
5 egg yolks, large
6 ounces (¾ cup) scant sugar
1 pound (4 sticks) unsalted butter, soft
4 ounces Praliné Paste (recipe, page 248)

Decoration:

confectioners' sugar

Hazelnut-Coffee Sauce:

6 ounces (¾ cup) freshly brewed strong coffee
3 tablespoons Liquid Caramel Flavoring (recipe, page 238)
4 ounces Praliné Paste (recipe, page 248)
1 tablespoon dark rum

Preheat oven to 220°F. Line a baking sheet with baking parchment. With a pencil, draw two 8-inch circles on the parchment, using a cake pan as a guide. Turn the paper over so that the graphite does not come off onto your meringue.

TO MAKE MERINGUE LAYERS: Place egg whites in bowl of electric mixer and whip until soft peaks form. Slowly add granulated sugar while beating at low speed. Increase speed to medium-high and whip until stiff peaks form. Sift confectioners' sugar and almond meal together into a bowl and stir in the milk. Quickly fold into egg whites and transfer the mixture to a pastry bag fitted with a plain ½-inch round tip. Pipe out two 8-inch circles on the baking parchment, starting at the center and spiraling outward. Bake for 1½ to 2 hours, or until meringue layers are crisp and dry. Remove from baking parchment and cool on racks.

TO PREPARE BUTTERCREAM: Place milk in a saucepan and bring to a boil. In the meantime, beat egg yolks and sugar until light and lemon-colored. Whisk a little of the boiling milk into the egg yolks and then pour entire mixture back into the saucepan. Do not allow it to boil again or the egg yolks will become grainy. Whisk constantly over moderate heat until mixture thickens and reaches 165°F. on a candy thermometer. (It should coat a spoon lightly.) Transfer custard to bowl of electric mixer and stir at low speed until cool. (If you do not have an electric mixer, transfer custard to a bowl and let cool, stirring occasionally so that a skin does not form; or slide a cube of cold butter across the surface. It will melt and leave a thin film.) Beat the soft butter into the custard a little at a time at low speed; then beat at high speed for 1 minute. Beat in the hazelnut paste. The cream should be very light and airy.

TO ASSEMBLE CAKE: Fill pastry bag fitted with plain ½-inch tube with hazelnut buttercream. Place one meringue layer on a cake board or a cardboard circle covered with tin foil. Pipe 1-inch balls, touching each other, around edge of meringue and then fill in the center area with a spiral of buttercream. Top with second layer of meringue, rounded side up, and press down very gently so as not to disturb balls of buttercream, which will show around the sides of the cake. Holding a plain ¼-inch tip on top of the larger one already on the pastry bag, pipe a simple multipetaled flower of buttercream at center of cake (see illustration). Sift a light layer of confectioners' sugar over entire top surface, flower included. The sugar will highlight the smooth meringue spirals.

HAZELNUT-COFFEE SAUCE: Combine the cold coffee, hazelnut paste, liquid caramel, and rum in a blender or food processor and blend until smooth. Transfer to a sauceboat and serve with the cake. *Serves 8.*

N O T E : All meringue layer cakes are susceptible to moisture and will eventually soften. However, the Noisette can be refrigerated for up to a day.

· · · ◊ · · ·

S N O W F L A K E

(Meringue Layer Cake with White Chocolate Mousse)

. . .

ADVANCED

This is a delicious combination of pale ivory meringue layers with a light, airy filling of white chocolate mousse. The outside of the cake is covered with "snowflakes."

8 egg whites, large
14 ounces (1½ cups) sugar
14 ounces (3½ cups) confectioners' sugar

White Chocolate Mousse:

4 ounces (½ cup) white chocolate
1½ ounces (3 tablespoons) unsalted butter, soft
8 ounces (1 cup) heavy cream

Preheat oven to 200°F. Line two baking sheets with baking parchment. With a pencil, draw three 8-by-5-inch ovals on the baking parchment; turn the paper over so the graphite does not get onto your meringue layers.

Place egg whites in bowl of electric mixer and whip until soft peaks form. Slowly add the granulated sugar while beating at low speed. Increase speed to medium-high and whip until stiff and glossy. Sift confectioners' sugar and lightly fold into egg whites. Transfer about two-thirds of the mixture to pastry bag. Pipe out three 8-inch ovals in a continuous spiral on prepared baking parchment. Add remaining meringue mixture to pastry bag and pipe long ½-inch rods or strips on empty half of the second baking sheet. (It is best to work with small quantities of meringue, as too much pressure exerted on the pastry bag will deflate the egg whites.) Transfer baking sheets to oven and bake for 1 hour or until meringue strips are crisp. Remove these by tearing off half the baking parchment and let cool. Continue baking the meringue ovals for another 1 to 2 hours or until dry. Let cool.

TO PREPARE WHITE CHOCOLATE MOUSSE: Cut chocolate into small pieces, place in a bowl, and melt over hot water. Let cool. Beat cream to soft peaks and refrigerate. Cream the butter until very light, then beat in cooled but still liquid chocolate. Fold in cream.

TO ASSEMBLE CAKE: Place one meringue layer on a cake board or a cardboard circle covered with tin foil and spread with one-fourth of the mousse. Top with second meringue layer and spread with another fourth of the mousse. Cover with third meringue layer, flat side up, and spread top and sides of cake with remaining mousse. Cut the strips of meringue into 1-inch to 2-inch sticks and use to cover top and sides of cake. (It is easiest to hold the cake on the palm of one hand at a slight angle over the supply of meringue sticks, and turn the cake slowly as you sprinkle.) *Serves 8.*

NOTE: All meringue preparations are susceptible to moisture and will eventually soften, but the Snowflake can be refrigerated for up to a day.

· · · ◊ · · ·

12

Christmas Specialties

. . . ◇ . . .

Christmas is a time to make extra-special, traditional delicacies—it's part of the ritual. In France, no holiday feast would be complete without the Bûche de Noël, or Christmas Log, a rolled sponge cake filled with butter-cream and covered with chocolate bark. It is always lavishly decorated with meringue mushrooms, trailing vines of pale green buttercream, and mar-zipan acorns and holly leaves, and there should be a pair of little meringue boots, because in Europe Saint Nicholas leaves gifts in boots or shoes, not stockings. Across the channel the British celebrate with their version of Christmas cake at teatime: a rich fruitcake covered with marzipan and snow-white Royal Icing. In Italy, it is de rigueur to eat Panettone (a light and airy lemon-peel and raisin-studded bread) during the holidays, accompanied by coffee or a glass of wine.

Here in the United States, we can make our own choice, or bake them all. Chocolate-dipped candied orange peel, dark and milk chocolate truffles, a rich chestnut and chocolate log, marzipan and apricot stuffed prunes are other possibilities . . . and make gifts that will be appreciated and remembered.

Index:

· · · ◇ · · ·

Christmas Specialties

PANETTONE

(Italian Fruit Loaf)

* * *

INTERMEDIATE

Panettone, the famous Christmas bread of Milan, is a delectably light and airy domed loaf, well studded with raisins and candied lemon peel. I owe this excellent recipe to a talented young Italian-American colleague, Gary Ruffia, who is passionately interested in conserving and refining the authentic, classic breads and pastries of Italy.

For this bread we use baker's compressed yeast (not the granular kind) and make a yeast "mother" in order to get two fermentations and superior results. The dough must be very well kneaded to develop fully the gluten in the flour, so I do recommend that you use an electric mixer. As I have explained in the yeast-dough section, professional bakeries have proofing boxes or special cupboards with controlled heat and humidity for raising the dough. I suggest that you heat your oven slightly, to 100°F., then turn it off. Put in your dough and alongside it a bowl of boiling water. Replenish the water once or twice, and you will provide a warm, moist atmosphere for the yeast. Alternatively, simply place the dough and the bowl of boiling water on a countertop and cover both with a cardboard box. This is a bit rustic, but it works.

This is a large recipe, making four 1¹/₄-pound loaves, but we have found that the texture of the bread is not as good when making only two loaves—the dough hook does not work as efficiently with so small an amount. In any case, Panettone makes a wonderful gift, and it freezes well.

1¾ pounds (5¾ cups) all-purpose flour
2 ounces baker's compressed yeast
1 pint (2 cups) water, room temperature
½ ounce (2 teaspoons) salt
5 ounces (1¼ sticks) unsalted butter, melted
5 ounces (⅔ cup) scant sugar
4 egg yolks, large
4 teaspoons orange extract
4 teaspoons vanilla extract
12 ounces (2 cups) dark raisins
12 ounces (2 cups) Candied Lemon Peel, diced (recipe, page
   215), or use store-bought variety

Place *half* the flour and *half* the yeast in bowl of electric mixer. Add *half* the water. Blend with a wooden spoon to incorporate, then mix with a dough hook for 5 minutes. Form mixture into a ball and place on a floured baking sheet or in a greased, warmed bowl. Cover with greased plastic wrap and let proof in a warm place until doubled in bulk, about 45 minutes. This preliminary step creates the yeast "mother," which in former times would have been saved from the previous day's baking.

Wash and dry mixer bowl and dough hook to eliminate any traces of hardened dough. In bowl, combine remaining flour, yeast, water, salt, lukewarm butter, sugar, egg yolks, and orange and vanilla extracts. Add the yeast mother and knead with a dough hook at medium speed until smooth and elastic, about 20 minutes. (This dough requires a great deal of kneading.) Add raisins and lemon peel. Remove from bowl and knead dough lightly on a floured surface for a minute or two. Let rest at room temperature for 15 minutes.

Have ready four 6-inch-diameter by 3½-inch-high steel cake rings. (These loaves should be tall and cylindrical in shape.) If rings are unobtainable, substitute 6-inch-diameter charlotte molds and be sure to line the bottoms with baking parchment. Line your rings with bands of baking parchment cut to extend 1 inch above the top rim and place on a heavy baking sheet covered with parchment paper.

Divide dough in four and form into balls. Center in pans and let rise in a warm place until trebled in bulk, about 1 to 1½ hours.

Preheat oven to 350°F. With a razor blade, slash a large X in the top of each loaf. Bake for approximately 40 minutes, until well risen and dark golden-brown. Unmold and let cool on racks. Cut in wedges to serve. *Makes four 1¼-pound loaves.*

. . . ◊ . . .

BÛCHE DE NOËL

(French Christmas Log)

· · ·

ADVANCED

Always served in France at Christmas time, the Yule Log traditionally consists of a rolled sponge cake garnished with buttercream bark and lavishly decorated with edible woodland trimmings: mushrooms, acorns, and leaves. It's best to make these a day or two before the cake is to be assembled—extra mushrooms in particular make attractive gifts when packed in small baskets.

Cake:

Traditional Sponge Roll sheet cake (recipe, page 128)

Rum Syrup:

5 ounces (⅝ cup) Simple Syrup (recipe, page 237), combined with
5 ounces (⅝ cup) dark rum

Buttercream:

6 cups Buttercream I (double recipe, page 107)
2 tablespoons Cointreau
8 ounces semisweet chocolate, melted
green food coloring

Decoration:

Meringue Mushrooms (page 199)
Marzipan Acorns (page 247)
Marzipan Leaves (page 246)
Meringue Shoes (page 199) (optional)
confectioners' sugar

Prepare two sheet cakes according to the recipe. Unmold onto racks and cool in the usual manner. Save one for another use. Trim crisp edges off the other sheet cake, which would prevent it from rolling properly.

Prepare buttercream and flavor with Cointreau. Transfer one-third, or about 2 cups, to a separate bowl and mix with melted and cooled chocolate.

Brush cake with rum syrup. Spread with 1½ cups of the white buttercream and roll up, starting from one of the long sides. Put on a cake board and place in freezer for 30 minutes to make cake easier to handle. When well chilled, cut a slanted slice from each end, about ½-inch high at one side and 1½-inches high at the other. Angle the knife so that the cut surfaces at each end of the log face upward slightly, which makes them easier to decorate. Place the cut pieces on top of the log to represent sawn-off branches. Coat log and sides of branches with a thin layer of chocolate buttercream. Freeze cake for 10 minutes.

Place remaining white buttercream in a pastry bag fitted with a plain round ½-inch tube. Pipe an outer rim and an inner disk on the cut surfaces of the log and branches. Squeeze buttercream remaining in bag into a small bowl and reserve. Put a small quantity of chocolate buttercream in a second pastry bag and pipe a second circle on the cut surfaces of the log, between the outer circle and the center disk. The entire surface should be covered. (The buttercream will be trimmed later to simulate "rings" within the tree trunk.) Freeze cake for 10 minutes. Coat log with remaining chocolate buttercream, using a fork to make lines imitating tree bark. Return to freezer for 20 minutes.

Tint leftover white buttercream with a tiny spot of green food coloring. Apply with the end of a toothpick—you want a very pale green. Place in a paper cone and snip a very small piece off the end to form a little hole.

Remove cake from freezer. Using a knife dipped in hot water and quickly dried, trim the buttercream on the four sawn-off portions of the log, leaving smooth surfaces. Pipe four or five green "vine stems" along the length of the log. Then snip a little more off the end of paper cone to make a flat slit. Pipe little leaves here and there along the vine stems. Arrange mushrooms, marzipan acorns, and marzipan leaves on top of log, and place meringue boots, if used, at one side. Return cake to refrigerator until required. It will keep for two or three days. Before serving, dust with a little confectioners' sugar to simulate snow. *Serves 12.*

. . . ◊ . . .

CHOCOLATE TRUFFLES
. . .

INTERMEDIATE

Chocolate truffles are supposed to resemble the "black diamonds" of French cuisine—the highly aromatic, dense, dark-brown fungus that sometimes grows underground near oak trees. Those of the Périgord region are especially prized. They are sniffed out by trained pigs or, less romantically perhaps, by dogs, and are astronomically expensive. These wild truffles are more or less round and are covered with earth when dug up, so we dust chocolate truffles with cocoa in imitation.

2¼ pounds bittersweet chocolate for filling, or ganache
1 pint (2 cups) milk, boiling
4 ounces (1 stick) unsalted butter, soft
4 ounces (½ cup) Grand Marnier or dark rum
1½ pounds bittersweet chocolate for dipping
unsweetened cocoa powder

Chop chocolate into small pieces and place in a bowl. Pour milk on top and stir. When smooth, stir in butter and Grand Marnier or rum. Refrigerate until stiff enough to pipe.

Fit a pastry bag with a plain ½-inch round tube and line a baking sheet with aluminum foil. Pipe chocolate filling into 1-inch mounds onto prepared baking sheet and refrigerate until very firm, about 2 hours.

TO TEMPER CHOCOLATE FOR COATING: Cut up chocolate and place in the top of a double boiler. Melt over hot water to between 122° and 131°F. on a candy thermometer. Spread about half the chocolate onto a marble slab or a cool, clean baking sheet.

Work it back and forth with a metal pastry scraper until it starts to thicken but not crystallize. Return to container with remaining melted chocolate and reheat to between 88° and 90°F. The tempered chocolate should have a nice sheen and be very smooth.

Roll the balls of chocolate filling with your fingers to make them completely round. Using a small fork, dip into tempered chocolate one at a time. Set dipped truffles onto aluminum foil—the filling, or ganache, is very cold, and the coating will set almost immediately. When all the truffles are dipped, dust with powdered cocoa. *Makes approximately 5 pounds.*

· · ◊ · · ·

C A N D I E D
O R A N G E P E E L
. . .

Once you have tasted your own aromatic candied peel, I guarantee that you will never again want to use the commercial variety—the difference is just too great!

6 medium oranges
2 cups water
1 pound (2 cups) generous sugar
2 tablespoons Grand Marnier (optional)

Cut a small slice off the top and bottom of each orange. Make 4 vertical cuts, through peel only, at equal intervals. Pull off the skin in four quarters, reserving the fruit for another use. Place peel in a pan and cover with cold water. Bring to a boil and then drain. Repeat this step twice more, to remove bitterness, and set aside. If the white pith is very thick, pare off some of it, but do not remove it all or the peel will become hard when candied.

Combine sugar with 2 cups water and bring to a boil. Let boil for 5 minutes and then add drained peel. Simmer gently for 1 hour. Place peel in a glass jar and cover with syrup, or syrup mixed with Grand Marnier if used. Store in the refrigerator. When required, drain well and then chop.

. . . ◊ . . .

CANDIED LEMON AND GRAPEFRUIT PEEL

. . .

Substitute the peel from 8 lemons or 4 grapefruit. (Tangerines are less satisfactory, as they have very little protective white pith.)

. . . ◊ . . .

SUGAR-COATED ORANGE AND GRAPEFRUIT PEEL

. . .

Drain the candied peel well and cut into matchsticks. Roll in sugar and let dry overnight on a rack. If desired, dip one end of each baton in dark chocolate and allow to harden.

. . . ◊ . . .

FRUITCAKE I
(American)

. . .

E A S Y

This is a good dark fruitcake that keeps well. The quantities given make about 4 pounds of cake, which can be baked in small or large loaf pans, ring molds, or round cake pans. The pans should be filled almost to the top, as the batter does not rise significantly. (To measure the capacity of various cake pans, fill them with water.) Naturally, smaller cakes will bake more quickly, so start testing after 45 minutes.

Fruit:

1 pound (2⅔ cups) diced mixed Candied Peel (recipe, page 214)
8 ounces (1⅓ cups) dark raisins, coarsely chopped
4 ounces (⅔ cup) currants
4 ounces (⅔ cup) figs or dates, chopped
4 ounces (⅔ cup) candied cherries
4 ounces (⅔ cup) blanched almonds
3 ounces (½ cup) pecan pieces
2 tablespoons Cognac
2 tablespoons orange marmalade

Ground Spices:

1 teaspoon cinnamon
¼ teaspoon allspice
1 teaspoon nutmeg
¼ teaspoon cloves

Batter:

4 ounces (1 stick) unsalted butter
4 ounces (½ cup) packed dark brown sugar
2 ounces (¼ cup) molasses

3 eggs, large

4 ounces (¾ cup) scant flour

½ teaspoon salt

Decoration:

additional candied cherries, nuts (optional)

Preheat oven to 325°F. Grease four 1-pound loaf pans or other size pans of choice, and line with parchment paper. Or use disposable aluminum foil pans.

In a large bowl, combine diced peel, raisins, currants, figs or dates, candied cherries, almonds, pecans, Cognac, marmalade, and spices.

In bowl of electric mixer, beat butter and brown sugar together until light and creamy. Beat in molasses. Add eggs one at a time, beating after each addition. Add flour and salt and mix until combined. Pour batter over fruit mixture and mix well. Transfer mixture to prepared pans and smooth the tops, decorating with additional halved candied cherries and nuts if desired. Bake for 1 to 1½ hours or until a cake tester inserted in the center comes out clean. Let cakes cool in pans. *Makes four 1-pound loaves, each serving 8.*

· · · ◇ · · ·

FRUITCAKE II

(American)

. . .

E A S Y

The quality of this cake depends on the fruit, so try to find choice candied orange peel, lemon peel, and citrus rind that is in halves or very large pieces, or make your own if possible (page 214). The bulk candied diced peel generally available in supermarkets is not really suitable for this cake. Imported French angelica, a pale-green candied root of delicate flavor, is available at specialty shops.

Allow three weeks for macerating the fruit in Cognac, and let the baked cakes mellow, tightly covered, for at least a week before serving.

Fruit:

3 pounds (8 cups) candied fruit (use an assortment, to taste, of
    citrus peel, melon rind, pineapple, candied cherries,
    and angelica)
Cognac to cover

Batter:

6 ounces (1¼ cups) scant all-purpose flour
3½ ounces (½ cup) scant sugar
3½ ounces (¾ stick plus 1 tablespoon) unsalted butter
3 whole eggs, large
1 teaspoon vanilla extract

Nuts:

4 ounces (1 cup) walnut pieces
4 ounces (1 cup) pecan pieces
additional candied cherries and almonds for decoration

Cover your selection of candied fruits and peels with Cognac and let steep for three weeks, covered.

Preheat oven to 300°F. and have ready five 7-by-3½-by-2-inch aluminum foil loaf pans.

In bowl of electric mixer, combine *half* the flour, the sugar, and butter. Beat for 5 minutes. Add eggs, vanilla, and remaining flour and beat at medium speed for 3 minutes. Remove bowl from stand.

Drain fruit and reserve the Cognac. Cut larger pieces of candied fruit into chunks. (Do not cut into small dice.) Stir fruit and nuts into batter. Divide mixture between the five loaf pans and smooth the tops. Decorate with halved candied cherries and pecans. Bake for 1½ hours or until a skewer inserted in the center of cake comes out clean. Remove from oven and brush liberally with reserved Cognac. Let cool in the pans. *Makes five 14-ounce fruitcakes.*

. . . ◊ . . .

F R U I T C A K E I I I
(English)

. . .

E A S Y

Even people who "don't like fruitcake" enjoy the English variety, which is a form of rich pound cake studded with fruit, as opposed to lots of fruit held together with a minimum of cake. In Britain, Christmas cake is always coated with a layer of marzipan and finished with Royal Icing and is usually round or square, never loaf-shaped.

Batter:

8 ounces (2 sticks) lightly salted butter
8 ounces (1 cup) packed dark brown sugar
5 eggs, large
10 ounces (2 cups) all-purpose flour
¼ teaspoon ground cloves
½ teaspoon ground cinnamon
½ teaspoon ground nutmeg
grated zest (colored part only) of half orange
grated zest (colored part only) of half lemon
2 ounces (½ cup) ground almonds

Fruit:

12 ounces (2 cups) currants
12 ounces (2 cups) dark raisins, coarsely chopped
12 ounces (2 cups) yellow raisins, coarsely chopped
8 ounces (1⅓ cups) mixed diced candied peel
2 ounces (⅓ cup) candied cherries
1 tablespoon Cognac
1 tablespoon rum

Decoration (optional):

8 ounces (1 cup) Apricot Glaze (recipe, page 241)
2 pounds Marzipan (recipe, page 243)
2¼ pounds Royal Icing (recipe, page 240)
1-inch-wide red ribbon; holly sprig

Preheat oven to 325°F. Grease a 9-inch springform pan and line with baking parchment.

In bowl of electric mixer, beat butter and sugar together until light and creamy. Beat in eggs one at a time. Sift flour, cloves, cinnamon, and nutmeg onto a sheet of wax paper and set aside. Add orange and lemon zest and ground almonds to mixer bowl, and then lightly stir in the flour and spices.

In a separate bowl, combine the currants, raisins, candied peel, candied cherries, Cognac, and rum. Stir into batter and mix well. Transfer to prepared pan and smooth the top. Bake for approximately 2 hours, until a tester inserted in the center comes out clean. Let cool in pan for 15 minutes before turning out onto a rack and peeling off the paper.

When completely cold, brush top and sides of cake, which should be smooth or bottom side up, with Apricot Glaze. Place on a cake board and let set, preferably overnight. Roll marzipan out evenly between two sheets of plastic wrap and cover the top and sides of the cake. Smooth with a rolling pin to make it very even, and make a right angle at the top edge. Store cake in an airtight tin for at least a week, or a month if desired, to let flavors mellow. When ready to decorate, coat with Royal Icing, making the surface completely smooth. When this has set hard, pipe a row of shells or stars around the edge and base of the cake. Put a sprig of real holly on top, and tie a red ribbon around the sides. *Serves 16 or more.*

· · · ◇ · · ·

DUNDEE FRUITCAKE

(Scottish)

· · ·

E A S Y

Though not technically a Christmas cake, this traditional Scottish fruitcake is made for special occasions and deserves inclusion here. This is quite an old recipe, and like other traditional fruitcakes, was made long before seedless raisins were introduced. Before then, each raisin had to be cut open and the seeds removed. This was laborious, but it released the flavor, and the slight stickiness of the cut raisins helped to hold the cake together when sliced. For these two reasons, it is a good idea to chop seedless raisins when using them in fruitcakes.

Batter:

8 ounces (2 sticks) lightly salted butter
8 ounces (1 cup) packed light brown sugar
4 eggs, large
2 ounces (½ cup) ground almonds
10 ounces (2 cups) all-purpose flour
½ teaspoon baking powder

Fruit:

4 ounces (⅔ cup) currants
4 ounces (⅔ cup) dark raisins, coarsely chopped
4 ounces (⅔ cup) yellow raisins, coarsely chopped
grated zest (colored part only) of 1 lemon
2 tablespoons Scotch whisky
2 ounces (¼ cup) milk

Decoration:

24 blanched almonds

Preheat oven to 325°F. Grease an 8-inch-diameter by 2-inch-high cake pan and line with baking parchment, which should extend 1 inch above rim (or use a springform pan).

Place butter and sugar in bowl of electric mixer and beat until light and fluffy. Beat in eggs one at a time and add the ground almonds. Sift the flour with salt and baking powder. Add to mixture, mixing until just combined. Remove bowl from mixer stand and fold in fruit and grated zest. Stir in whisky and milk. Transfer mixture to prepared pan and make a slight hollow in the center so that the cake will rise without a peak in the middle. Arrange almonds on top of cake in a larger outer and a smaller inner circle. Bake for 1½ to 2 hours or until a tester inserted in the center of the cake comes out clean. Let cake cool in pan for 15 minutes before turning out on a rack to cool. *Serves 10 to 12.*

PRUNEAUX FOURRÉS
DE TOURS

(Stuffed Glazed Prunes)

. . .

INTERMEDIATE

Tours, my hometown, has been famous for prunes for hundreds of years. The monks of the abbey of Clairac, near Bordeaux, perfected the art of drying the local plums as far back as the sixteenth century, and as coincidence would have it, the prunes of my boyhood home are readily available to me here in California—cuttings of the local plum were first imported in 1856 by a Frenchman named Louis Pellier.

To stuff prunes, it is important that they be malleable and readily molded into their original oval shape. Modern processing renders them soft, but it is still a good idea to plunge the prunes in boiling water for a couple of minutes before filling them, as they are often still slightly leathery. The fillings should not be too sweet, and should be heightened with some good liqueur. The stuffed prunes are at their best when glazed with a thin layer of very light caramel, but must be served the same day or the glaze will lose its crackle. The stuffed prunes keep well, so make them ahead of time and glaze only as many as required shortly before serving. Two cups of glaze is about the minimum possible for dipping the prunes.

24 ounces (2 packages, about 80) soft pitted prunes, large size

Filling #1:

6 ounces Marzipan (recipe, page 243)
1 tablespoon Kirsch
green food coloring

Filling #2:

4 ounces dried apricots
3 ounces (⅓ cup) generous sugar
1 tablespoon apricot brandy

Filling #3:

4 ounces soft pitted prunes
3 ounces (⅓ cup) generous sugar
1 tablespoon rum

Glaze:

1 pound (2 cups) generous sugar
⅔ cup water

Parboil the prunes in boiling water for 2 minutes, and drain well. Slit each prune along one side.

TO MAKE MARZIPAN FILLING: In bowl of food processor, combine cut-up marzipan, Kirsch, and 1 drop of green food coloring. Process until evenly blended, then knead by hand until smooth. Roll into oval nuggets and insert into prunes so that an almond shape of filling shows through the slit. Make a crisscross design on the marzipan with a knife. Fills about 25 prunes.

TO MAKE APRICOT FILLING: Poach apricots in water to cover until soft, about 20 minutes. Drain and place in bowl of food processor with sugar. Process until pureed. The mixture will turn opaque. Return to pan and stir with a wooden spoon over low heat until it thickens slightly and turns a clear orange color once more. Stir in apricot brandy. When cool enough to handle, transfer to a pastry bag fitted with a plain ½-inch tip and fill prunes. Mold with wet fingers into neat ovals. Fills about 25 prunes.

TO MAKE PRUNE FILLING: Follow procedure for apricot filling but substitute prunes and rum. Fills about 25 prunes.

TO MAKE GLAZE: Place sugar in a heavy saucepan, preferably of un-lined copper, with ⅔ cup water. Bring to a boil and let cook until it reaches 300°F. on a candy thermometer. Remove from heat or this very light caramel will darken and become too thick. Impale a stuffed prune on the tines of a dipping fork (or cradle between two table forks) and dip quickly into the syrup. Place on a sheet of oiled alu-minum foil to dry—the syrup will harden almost immediately.

. . . ◇ . . .

G Â T E A U   M A R R O N

(Chestnut Log)

. . .

E A S Y

This rich confection is made with imported French chestnut purée, which is available in cans from fancy food stores and some supermarkets.

1 pound 2 ounce-can imported canned sweetened chestnut purée
8 ounces (2 sticks) unsalted butter, at room temperature
3 ounces (⅓ cup) generous sugar
4 ounces bittersweet chocolate, melted
1 tablespoon Cognac
6 ounces bittersweet chocolate, for glaze
4 ounces (½ cup) sweet almond oil or light, flavorless vegetable oil
6 ounces Marzipan (recipe, page 243), for decoration
½ cup buttercream (see below)
green food coloring

In bowl of electric mixer, combine chestnut purée, butter, and sugar and mix with paddle at slow speed. Add melted and cooled but still liquid chocolate and Cognac. Mix until smooth. Turn mixture out onto a sheet of plastic wrap and form into a log, 12 inches long by 3½ inches in diameter. Pat into shape with a rubber spatula; then roll up, using the plastic wrap to help you. Place on a cake board (or cardboard covered with foil) and freeze until firm, 30 to 60 minutes.

Melt chocolate for glaze over hot water and set aside. To make marzipan chestnuts for decoration, roll marzipan into 1¼-inch balls and dip in melted chocolate. Make two or three and place on a sheet of aluminum foil and let set. In the meantime, tint a quarter cup of buttercream a very pale green with food coloring. (If you have no buttercream made up, cream together equal quantities of unsalted butter and confectioners' sugar.) Place buttercream in a small paper cone and set aside. To make marzipan chestnut leaves, knead the remaining marzipan with a spot of green food coloring to make it a very pale green. Roll out on a marble slab dusted with confectioners' sugar (or between two sheets of plastic wrap) and cut out two or three chestnut leaves (see illustration).

To glaze cake, combine melted chocolate with the oil. Remove plastic wrap and pour glaze over chestnut log, covering any missed areas at the sides with the help of a spatula. Work fast, as the glaze will set up quickly on the cold log. Neaten edges where glaze runs onto the cake board. If necessary, return cake to freezer until glaze is set.

Transfer the log to a suitable serving platter. Place one of the chocolate-covered marzipan balls on top of the cake, securing it with a dab of melted chocolate. Pipe two thin lines of buttercream from the top to the bottom of the ball, forming a pointed oval. This represents the typical slit in a chestnut's outer husk. Cover the remaining surface with "chestnut prickles" or little points of buttercream. Repeat with the remaining balls of marzipan, arranging them in a group with the marzipan leaves. Refrigerate the log until serving time. *Serves 12.*

N O T E : I recommend offering Ladyfingers (recipe, page 135) with this gâteau, as it is rich, and the plain sponge fingers make a good contrast.

13.

Reduced-Calorie Cakes

· · · ◇ · · ·

You might wonder why a dedicated pastry chef would want to make low-calorie cakes—it sounds like a contradiction in terms! As a matter of fact, I do not believe that my creations are fattening when eaten in moderation. I sample them all day long and do not gain weight, but of course I must admit to being very active. I think it is far more satisfactory to enjoy a reasonable amount of the very best pâtisserie, made from the very finest ingredients, than to insult your palate with mass-produced junk food, loaded with sugar and fat. Top-quality desserts, on the other hand, can be savored for their delicate contrasting flavors, textures, and enticing appearance, and are not cloyingly sweet.

Nonetheless, many people are concerned about limiting their intake of fats and sugars, and creating the desserts in this chapter was an enjoyable challenge. All three are light and delicate, with wonderful textures, and your guests will never guess that these cakes are low in calories unless you choose to tell them. Using my "basic building blocks" of plain sponge cake, meringue, yogurt, fruit, and a minimum of sugar, I hope you will be inspired to try your own combinations.

Index:

$\cdots \diamond \cdots$

Reduced-Calorie Cakes

REDUCED-CALORIE PINEAPPLE MOUSSE CAKE

. . .

INTERMEDIATE

I recommend making the sponge cake the day before the cake is to be assembled, but it is not absolutely necessary.

Cake:

3 egg whites, large
3 ounces (⅓ cup) generous sugar
2 egg yolks, large
½ teaspoon vanilla extract
2½ ounces (½ cup) all-purpose flour
¼ teaspoon baking powder

Filling:

1 20¼-ounce-can pineapple rings in natural juice
1 tablespoon sugar
2 tablespoons fresh lemon juice
¼ ounce (1 envelope) unflavored gelatin
2 tablespoons cold water
1 pint (2 cups) low-fat plain yogurt
1 tablespoon dark rum

Decoration:

6 fresh raspberries

Preheat oven to 350°F. Butter an 8-inch cake pan.

Place eggs whites in bowl of electric mixer and whisk until soft peaks form. Slowly add 2 tablespoons of the sugar and continue whisking until stiff and glossy. Transfer meringue to a separate bowl. Place yolks, remaining sugar, and vanilla in mixer bowl. Beat at high speed until light, thick, and pale in color. Sift flour and baking powder together onto a sheet of wax paper. Fold half the egg whites into the sugar and egg-yolk emulsion, then fold in flour. Fold in remaining egg whites. Spread batter evenly into prepared pan. Bake for 15 to 20 minutes, until golden and springy to the touch. Unmold onto rack and let cool.

Place cake on a flat plate. Make a collar of a double thickness of aluminum foil extending 2 inches above cake and secure tightly around it with sticky tape. Drain pineapple and reserve juice. In a small saucepan, combine 6 ounces of the pineapple juice with the lemon juice and sugar and heat to boiling. (Reserve fruit and remaining juice.) Combine gelatin with cold water and immediately add to the boiling juice. Remove from heat and stir for a few seconds. Pour mixture into a bowl and let cool to lukewarm. Let mixture stand until it starts to thicken—it should have the consistency of unbeaten egg whites. (You can hasten the process by placing in the freezer for a few minutes, but check and stir often or the mixture will set up.) Whisk in the yogurt and add the rum.

Reserve 3 pineapple rings for decoration and chop the remainder. Top cake with pineapple and any remaining juice. Cover with yogurt mixture. Refrigerate until set, about 1 hour. When ready to serve, run a knife blade around inside of aluminum foil collar and remove it. Decorate top of cake with half circles of pineapple, placing them around the edge. Center a raspberry inside each half circle. *Serves 8, at approximately 185 calories per serving.*

· · · ◇ · · ·

REDUCED-CALORIE
SUMMER DÉLICE
. . .

3 egg whites, large

6 ounces (¾ cup) scant sugar, for meringue

2 ounces (¼ cup) generous sugar, for custard

4 ounces (½ cup) cold water

3 egg yolks, large

¼ ounce (1 envelope) plain unflavored gelatin

½ teaspoon vanilla extract

6 ounces (¾ cup) low-fat plain yogurt

2 ounces (¼ cup) sour cream

6 ounces (1 cup) fresh berries (use one type or a combination of raspberries, small strawberries, and blueberries)

1 teaspoon unsweetened cocoa powder

Preheat oven to 200°F. Line a baking sheet with baking parchment, and draw a 9-inch circle on the underside of the paper. Fit a pastry bag with a ½-inch plain round tip.

In bowl of electric mixer, whisk egg whites until soft peaks start to form. Slowly add *half* (3 ounces) of the sugar, then beat at high speed until meringue is stiff and glossy. Remove bowl from stand and fold in the remaining 3 ounces sugar, one-third at a time. Transfer mixture to pastry bag. Starting at center of circle, pipe a tight spiral of meringue to form the 9-inch-diameter base. Smooth with a spatula if necessary to form an even layer. To make sides, pipe two circles around the edge of the base, one inside the other and touching each other. Pipe a third circle on top of the other two, pyramid fashion. Bake meringue case for 1½ to 2 hours, until dry and crisp.

Dissolve sugar in 2 ounces (¼ cup) water and boil for 2 minutes to make a simple syrup. Let cool to lukewarm. Place egg yolks and simple syrup in top of double boiler. Whisk vigorously over simmering water until custard thickens, about 7 minutes. Place gelatin in a small pan and add 2 ounces (¼ cup) cold water. Let soak for a few minutes, then heat to simmering point, stirring constantly. Stir into custard and add vanilla. Let mixture cool until just starting to set. (Process can be hastened if mixture is placed in freezer for a few minutes, but check and stir frequently.) Fold in yogurt. Gently stir in berries and pour into meringue shell. Chill until set, about 2 hours. Sift cocoa lightly over surface before serving. *Serves 8, at approximately 150 calories per serving.*

· · · ◊ · · ·

REDUCED-CALORIE
PEAR SOUFFLÉ CAKE
· · ·

Here, a light sponge cake is spread thinly with jam, rolled up, and then sliced to form the sides of the dessert. The base is covered with a circle of the same sponge and topped with diced pears. A delicate pear mousse fills the cake shell.

Cake:

5 egg whites, large
3½ ounces (½ cup) scant sugar
3 egg yolks, large
3½ ounces (⅔ cup) generous all-purpose flour
½ teaspoon baking powder
3 tablespoons raspberry jam

Filling:

2 16-ounce cans pears, packed in pear juice
3 egg yolks, large
2 ounces (¼ cup) generous sugar
¼ ounce (1 envelope) unflavored gelatin
2 tablespoons water
3 egg whites, large
8 ounces (1 cup) low-fat plain yogurt

Preheat oven to 425°F. Line a 17-by-12-inch sheet cake pan with baking parchment.

In bowl of electric mixer, whisk egg whites until starting to form soft peaks. Slowly add *half* the sugar and continue beating until mixture is stiff and glossy. Transfer to a separate container. Add egg yolks and remaining sugar to mixer bowl and whisk until pale and thick. Sift flour and baking powder together onto a sheet of wax paper. Remove bowl from stand and fold in half the egg whites, the flour, and the remaining egg whites. Spread evenly in prepared pan and bake for 10 minutes, until cake springs back to a light finger pressure. Unmold onto rack. Wait for 1 minute, then peel off baking parchment. As soon as cake is cold, cut out an 8-inch circle, using a cake pan as a guide, and set aside. From remaining sheet cake, cut an 11-by-8-inch rectangle, without including any crisp edges. Spread the smooth side with jam and immediately roll up tightly, starting from one of the short sides. Wrap in plastic and freeze for 1 hour, or overnight.

Place a 9-inch cake ring, or the rim from a springform pan, on a flat serving platter. (If using a springform pan rim, line with a collar of aluminum foil.) Cut the rolled cake into ⅓-inch-thick slices and line the sides of the cake ring. (Reserve leftover slices for another use.) Compress the sliced rounds slightly so that the top edge of the cake shell is flat. Place the reserved circle of cake in the bottom.

Drain pears and reserve juice—there will be 1½ cups. Heat juice to boiling point. Beat egg yolks and sugar until pale and thick, and whisk into pear juice. Whisk for a few seconds but do not let boil or the egg yolks will curdle. Remove from heat. Blend gelatin with water and immediately whisk into hot mixture. Place in blender or food processor with 4 pear halves and blend until smooth. Chill mixture until it starts to set up. (To hasten process, you can place in freezer, but check and stir frequently.)

Whisk egg whites until very stiff. Fold yogurt and egg whites into pear juice mixture. Reserve one pear half for decoration and dice the remainder. Place diced pears in cake shell and top with creamy mixture. Refrigerate cake for 4 hours. Run a sharp knife around sides and lift off ring. Slice reserved pear half thinly lengthwise, almost but not all the way through the stem end. Fan out slightly and place on top of cake. Keep refrigerated until serving time. *Serves 8, at approximately 225 calories per serving.*

14

Miscellaneous Preparations

. . . ◇ . . .

Index:

SUGAR COOKING

. . .

Always use enough water to completely dissolve sugar crystals when cooking: about one-third of the volume is usually sufficient. (If you add more no harm will be done, but you will have to boil the mixture for a longer time to evaporate the water.)

Sugar goes through a number of distinct stages when cooked, as follows:

220°F.	104°C.	jelly
240°F.	116°C.	soft ball
245°F.	118°C.	medium ball
250°F.	121°C.	hard ball
300°F.	149°C.	small crack
310°F.	154°C.	hard crack
325°F.	163°C.	golden crack
350°F.	177°C.	caramel

. . . ◊ . . .

SIMPLE SYRUP

. . .

EASY

This syrup, which is used extensively for saturating elaborate cakes and for poaching fruit, can be prepared in any quantity. The proportions of sugar and water are always one to one.

1 pound (2 cups) sugar
1 pint (2 cups) water

Heat sugar and water in a saucepan, stirring until sugar is dissolved, and let boil for 5 minutes. If adding flavoring, do so after the syrup has cooled. It will keep for a few days in the refrigerator, tightly covered. *Makes 2 cups.*

· · · ◊ · · ·

H E A V Y   S Y R U P
· · ·

E A S Y

1½ pounds (3 cups) generous sugar
1 pint (2 cups) water

Heat sugar and water in a saucepan, stirring until sugar is dissolved, and let boil for 5 minutes. *Makes 2½ cups.*

· · · ◊ · · ·

L I Q U I D   C A R A M E L
F L A V O R I N G
· · ·

E A S Y

8 ounces (1 cup) generous sugar
3 ounces (⅜ cup) water
1 tablespoon dark rum

Boil sugar and water to dark caramel stage, 350°F. on a candy thermometer. Remove from heat and add enough additional water (about 2 ounces or ¼ cup) to make a pouring liquid. Stir in rum. Stored airtight in the refrigerator, it will keep for one month. *Makes approximately 1 cup.*

FONDANT

· · ·

INTERMEDIATE

1½ pounds (3 cups) generous sugar
8 ounces (1 cup) water
¼ teaspoon cream of tartar

Lightly oil a marble slab or large metal baking sheet. Bring sugar, water, and cream of tartar to a boil, then wash any sugar crystals off sides of pan with a pastry brush dipped in water. Boil to 240°F. on a candy thermometer. Spread syrup onto slab and let cool for 10 minutes, until barely lukewarm. Work the mixture back and forth with a metal pastry scraper until the fondant becomes white and thick, which will take about 10 minutes. Store in an airtight plastic container, covering the surface with damp cheesecloth. Fondant will have the best sheen if allowed to stand overnight before using. Fondant will keep for several months.

To use for glazing purposes, heat gently over simmering water and add enough Simple Syrup (recipe, page 237) to thin to the consistency of heavy cream. Use only enough food coloring to make very pale pastel shades. Fondant glaze is used at about 98°F.

To make chocolate or coffee fondant, add melted unsweetened chocolate (25 percent to 50 percent of volume), or instant powdered coffee dissolved in a little hot water (1 to 2 teaspoons per cup of fondant) together with enough Simple Syrup to reach a coating consistency. *Makes approximately 3 cups.*

· · · ◇ · · ·

ROYAL ICING

. . .

This is the classic Royal Icing. A simpler version for use on Allumettes (recipe, page 77) can be made by combining confectioners' sugar with enough lightly beaten egg white to obtain a smooth, spreading consistency.

2 pounds (8 cups) confectioners' sugar
4 egg whites, large

Sift sugar twice. Stir egg whites lightly but not enough to make air bubbles. Add half the sugar and stir well. Beat for 5 minutes. Cover with several thicknesses of dampened cheesecloth and let stand for 30 minutes, to allow any air bubbles to rise to the surface. Gradually beat in remaining sugar until consistency is smooth and glossy.

If using Royal Icing to pipe cake decorations, add 1 tablespoon lemon juice. The citric acid will make it dry harder. *Makes about 2¹/₄ pounds.*

. . . ◇ . . .

QUICK FRUIT GLAZE

. . .

EASY

To make golden fruit glaze for apple tarts and so on, heat good-quality apricot jam and freshly squeezed lemon juice in the proportion of 1 cup jam to 1 tablespoon lemon juice. Strain and apply with a pastry brush.

To make red glaze, substitute raspberry or strawberry jam, depending on use. Omit lemon juice with raspberry jam; it has enough acidity.

TRADITIONAL APRICOT GLAZE

. . .

6½ pounds firm, ripe apricots
6½ pounds sugar
3 pints water
additional sugar

In a large, wide pan, preferably of unlined copper, combine whole fruit, sugar, and water. Let simmer for 20 minutes. Cut apricots in half and remove pits. Place fruit in a food mill and purée. Weigh the fruit pulp, and for each quart, add 1¼ pounds sugar. Return to rinsed pan and let simmer for 20 minutes.

Place in sterilized glass jars and cover tightly. It will keep in the refrigerator for four months or in the freezer for one year. *Makes approximately 12 quarts.*

. . . ◊ . . .

CHOCOLATE, TEMPERING FOR USE

. . .

ADVANCED

1½ pounds best-quality bittersweet chocolate

Cut up chocolate and place in the top of a double boiler. Melt over hot water to between 122° and 131°F. on a candy thermometer. Spread about half the chocolate onto a marble slab or a cool, clean baking sheet. Work it back and forth with a metal pastry scraper until it starts to thicken but not crystallize. Return to top of double boiler with remaining melted chocolate and reheat to between 88° and 90°F. on a candy thermometer. The tempered chocolate should have a nice sheen and be very smooth.

CHOCOLATE CURLS

. . .

ADVANCED

Spread 2 or 3 ounces of tempered chocolate onto marble in a narrow band about 4 inches wide and ⅛ inch thick. Allow to cool until it starts to set up, and the surface dulls. Holding a knife blade at a slight angle, scrape up narrow bands of chocolate, which will curl up as you go and form corkscrew curls. (It takes a little practice to judge when the chocolate is at the right temperature, but persevere.) Clean off marble and repeat with more chocolate. Place the completed chocolate curls on a plate and refrigerate until required.

. . . ◊ . . .

CHOCOLATE RUFFLES

. . .

ADVANCED

Spread 2 or 3 ounces of tempered chocolate onto marble in a narrow band about 4 inches wide and ⅛ inch thick. Allow to cool until it starts to set up and the surface dulls. Holding a palette knife or clean paint scraper at a slight angle, almost horizontal, scrape up a wide band of chocolate, from one end to the other. Hold your thumb against one edge of the chocolate ribbon, and they will ruffle up in a fan shape as you go along. As with making chocolate curls, this takes practice, but persevere. Clean off marble and repeat with more chocolate. Keep the chocolate ruffles chilled until required.

CHOCOLATE LEAVES

. . .

ADVANCED

Choose fresh rose or lemon leaves that have not been sprayed with pesticide. Wash and dry carefully. Holding each leaf by the stem, paint the top or shiny side with a thin layer of tempered chocolate, letting it drip off the pointed end. Place leaves on a sheet of aluminum foil and refrigerate until set. Carefully peel off the green leaf, and a chocolate leaf will remain, complete with veins.

. . . ◊ . . .

MARZIPAN

(Pâte d'Amandes Crue)

. . .

EASY

This is a good all-purpose almond paste to use for covering cakes, such as the Princess Cake (recipe, page 141), for stuffing dried fruits (recipe, page 224), and for making marzipan decorations. To blanch almonds, place in boiling water for 1 minute, drain, and let cool. Pop the nuts out of the skins.

1 pound (2 cups) generous sugar
8 ounces (1 cup) water
1 pound (2⅔ cups) almonds, blanched
3 pounds (12 cups) confectioners' sugar
5 ounces (⅝ cup) liquid glucose or light corn syrup

Combine sugar and water in a heavy pan and heat until clear. Let boil for 1 minute. Set aside. In bowl of food processor, combine almonds and confectioners' sugar. Grind until large crumbs are formed, then add liquid glucose and reserved sugar syrup. Continue processing until a smooth paste is formed. Store, covered and airtight, in the refrigerator. It will keep for one month. *Makes approximately 5½ pounds.*

· · · ◇ · · ·

QUICK MARZIPAN
· · ·

EASY

8 ounces (2 cups) powdered almonds
10 ounces (2½ cups) confectioners' sugar
3 egg whites, large

Combine almonds and confectioners' sugar and stir in the egg whites. Place mixture in a plastic bag and roll with a rolling pin, folding and rerolling until smooth. *Makes approximately 1¼ pounds.*

· · · ◇ · · ·

FINE MARZIPAN
(Pâte d'Amandes Cuite)
· · ·

INTERMEDIATE

1 pound (2 cups) generous sugar
5 ounces (⅝ cup) water
1 pound (3 cups) scant almonds, blanched
liquid glucose or light corn syrup

In an unlined copper pan, combine sugar and water and let boil to hard ball stage, 250°F. on a candy thermometer. Place almonds in a bowl and pour boiling sugar over them, mixing and turning the nuts. Let cool. Transfer to bowl of food processor and grind until large crumbs form. Add liquid glucose and continue processing until the mixture resembles fine powder. Freeze for 20 minutes, then repeat this process twice more. *Makes approximately 2 pounds.*

· · · ◇ · · ·

M A R Z I P A N   R O S E S
· · ·

A D V A N C E D

These are simple to make when you understand the technique. It doesn't hurt to have a real rose beside you when you first attempt to make them, so that you can study the configuration of the unfolding petals. Confectioners' sugar is added to the marzipan so that the roses will dry hard and hold their shape. Use red or yellow food coloring in very small quantities to make pink or pale-yellow roses.

Blend about 1 pound of marzipan with 25 percent, or 4 ounces, of confectioners' sugar and a drop or two of food coloring in a food processor. Roll into a long rope about 1 inch in diameter and cut off eight to ten ½-inch slices. Place between two sheets of plastic wrap and flatten the edges of each slice with your thumb into a large petal. The "petals" should look like a poached egg with the yolk off to one side, and the edges should be almost transparent. Fashion a pointed pedestal about 3 inches high and stick the base to your work surface. Roll one petal around the top, leaving an aperture at the top (to imitate the still-folded center of the flower) and attaching the base of the petal halfway down the pedestal. (See illustration.) Cup this center with two more petals, opposite each other, rolling one edge back slightly by flicking with your finger. Continue wrapping petals around the center until the rose is full-blown. Slice off at the base of the petals and leave to dry. Repeat with remaining marzipan, forming each one with eight to ten petals.

MARZIPAN LEAVES
. . .

ADVANCED

Add 25 percent of its weight in confectioners' sugar and a drop of green food coloring to your marzipan. Roll out ⅛ inch thick on a marble slab dusted with confectioners' sugar. Using a 1-inch-diameter round fluted cutter, cut out as many leaves as required. Elongate each leaf slightly by rolling gently with a rolling pin, and mark in veins by scoring lightly with a knife. To make two halves for each leaf, pinch gently at both ends between thumb and forefinger (see illustration). Pinch the edges of the leaves gently to make them thinner. Let leaves dry before storing airtight. To make straight-edged leaves, cut out pointed ovals with a knife and then mark with veins.

MARZIPAN ACORNS

· · ·

These do not require the addition of confectioners' sugar. Roll natural-colored marzipan into 1-inch balls. Elongate each ball into an oval. Dip each oval halfway in melted chocolate and then in chocolate sprinkles. Leave to set on a sheet of aluminum foil.

PRALINÉ PASTE, QUICK

· · ·

EASY

4 ounces (²/₃ cup) almonds
4 ounces (²/₃ cup) hazelnuts
1 ounce (2 tablespoons) Simple Syrup (recipe, page 237)
7 ounces (1³/₄ cups) approximately confectioners' sugar

Preheat oven to 400°F. Toss nuts with Simple Syrup and spread out on a large baking sheet. Bake for 15 to 20 minutes, until nicely toasted. Weigh the nuts and combine with an equal amount of confectioners' sugar. Grind in food processor and then freeze, using the same method as described for Traditional Praliné Paste (below) and repeating it three times. This paste will be slightly lighter in color but still of excellent flavor. *Makes approximately 14 ounces.*

PRALINÉ PASTE,
TRADITIONAL

. . .

INTERMEDIATE

This felicitous combination of toasted nuts and caramel is said to have been invented by a chef of the Maréchal du Plessis de Praslin, who was born in 1598 and lived to the ripe old age of seventy-seven. Along with fine liqueurs, it is one of the most delicious flavorings for buttercreams and chocolates. Praliné Paste will keep almost indefinitely in the refrigerator in an airtight jar.

8 ounces (1 cup) generous sugar
2½ ounces (5 tablespoons) water
4 ounces (⅔ cup) whole almonds, with skins
4 ounces (⅔ cup) whole hazelnuts, with skins

In a heavy pan of unlined copper or stainless steel, combine sugar and water. Let boil to the thread stage (very soft ball), 235°F. on a candy thermometer. Add nuts and stir well. Let cook for 5 to 10 minutes. The sugar will crystallize, like white sand, and the nuts will toast and turn golden inside. Keep stirring for about 5 minutes, breaking up any lumps. When the sugar melts again and turns into a light caramel, pour the mixture onto an oiled marble slab or oiled baking sheet. Let cool.

When the mixture is cold, break it up and place the pieces in bowl of food processor. Grind, in batches if necessary, until even crumbs form. Spread out on a baking sheet and transfer to freezer for 20 minutes. Repeat this grinding and freezing process twice more, until a very fine paste is formed. *Makes approximately 1½ cups, or 12 ounces.*

. . . ◊ . . .

Index

. . . ◇ . . .